The Wingless Fairy

C.H. LYN

Horizon Publishing

Contents

Once upon a time, eight hundred years before a prince set out to make a deal with a sea witch, there lived a feisty fairy, an adventurous orphan, and an ambitious pirate.

CHAPTER ONE

The Finest Trick

"Faster!" Tyl shouted, her small voice ringing through the air like a whistling bird as she flew backwards.

Pan darted forward, his dagger clenched in one hand, curved short-sword in the other.

The wide grin on Tyl's face didn't falter an inch as Pan's sword came within a hair of the corkscrew curls framing her face. The blade sliced through a thick chunk of vine, leaving an opening between large boughs for him to fly through.

"Ha," she cackled. "Missed me!"

"I'm not *trying* to hit you, Tyl." Pan rolled his eyes, still speeding after her.

He had a disadvantage. Well, several disadvantages, if Tyl was honest. His size was one—his lumbering human body in a forest grown for fairies. He didn't have wings, flying with pure fairy magic instead, and he hadn't been born in the air.

All of which counted for little when the two of them fought pirates or monsters, but absolutely mattered when it came to their races.

Tyl spun up, twisting gracefully between tree branches as she made for the open sky above them. Her gossamer wings glistened in the early morning light reflecting off the bay.

"Maybe you'd win for once if you did," she called.

Pan didn't respond.

Tyl broke through the leaves and paused. The world was frozen up here. Still and quiet. The clouds over the ocean were slowly burning off. The sun had come all the way up, the glowing orb looking as though it sat upon the water to the east.

The beach to the west was still dark, the light not quite reaching past the tall treetops. Pan's treehouse, a massive twisting thing on the southwestern edge of the island, was that pale green and grey it only was on foggy mornings.

Tyl frowned. She shouldn't have been able to look around for so long. Confusion swamped her small body and she twisted, searching for her friend.

"Pan?"

The confusion began to melt, replaced with quickening fear as her gaze turned north.

Then, out of the thick foliage beneath her, Pan burst from the leaves. He cupped her in his hands, his laughter echoing out over the forest as he spun with them both.

She tumbled in his hands, dizzy but relieved for a second. Then the anger hit, filling her up like a cup overflowing. She pulled her razorleaf thin sword from her hip and poked him in the thumb.

"Ouch! Tyl, it was just a trick." Pan released her, shaking his hand before pressing his thumb hard to stop the bleeding. "What was that for?"

She was red still, but the burst of anger eased away at the silly sight of him holding his thumb to his chest.

She tried to keep a straight face. "You scared me, Pan. That's not how a race works, and you know it."

He gave her an appraising look. "You're not even mad anymore, ha. Besides, it's been the same race forever, Tyl. I wanted to shake it up." He stuck his tongue out at her.

She mimicked him, and then flew to his side. "Gimme your thumb."

Pan opened his hand, and she landed on his palm. With slender fingers, Tyl brushed the tip of her delicate wings. The magic that coursed through them coated her dark amber skin and, with a quick mutter about cheating, she dabbed his thumb. The tiny slice healed in an instant.

Tyl held onto his thumb as Pan flew the two of them towards the great oak on the south end of the island. Not as tall as the Hollow, the towering set of twisting evergreens to the north, but still a beautiful tree.

They settled onto a favorite bough, and Pan dug into one of the many pouches tied to his ivy and twine belt.

"Are you really bored with the race?" Tyl asked as he tore a chunk of a slice of blueberry bread and passed it to her.

Pan shrugged a thin shoulder.

Tyl squinted, suspicious. "What is it, Pan?"

He leaned back, his golden brown curls brushing against the moss-covered bark of the oak trunk. His youthful face was a trick. One of the finest tricks the two of them had ever played.

Tyl wasn't big on keeping track of time. She celebrated the solstices at the Hollow like a good fairy. She and Pan threw birthday parties just about whenever they wanted—or whenever a Lost One had been with them for more than a few months.

She did know, however, that it had been many many years since she'd snuck a young Pan to the spring and clapped as he drank.

It had been funny. A silly lark. And it let him stay... which, in some small hidden part of Tyl's mind, she knew was the real reason behind doing it.

The law of the Hollow—the queen's law—was clear. Mankind was *not* allowed on the island.

So, it was lucky Pan was not yet a man.

Or, at least, it was lucky he'd not yet started growing a beard by the time the two of them had figured out a way to keep him there. The queen didn't need to know that a boy was considered a man by the time he was twenty. She also didn't need to know that humans aged over decades, not centuries.

However long it had been, one thing was certain. Pan was free to live on the island.

Maybe someday the queen would question why the boy had not aged a day in years and years. Then again, maybe not. She was quite a busy queen.

Tyl hefted her slice of bread and flew to Pan's knee. She perched there, legs crossed, wings drifting behind her. "Pan?"

He met her dark gaze with his bright hazel one. "I love the race, Tyl. I love the race, and the island, and the tree house, and you."

Tyl narrowed her eyes. "But?"

Pan ran a hand through his wavy curls. He stared out at the treehouse below them. The Lost Ones were starting to wake, rolling out of hammocks and off cots to begin a day of adventure.

His gaze traveled further, to the crystal blue waters surrounding the island. Half a smile and the glint in his eye gave him a somewhat wistful look.

After another second, he blinked, looked down at her, and cracked a full grin. "But nothing. Just tired this morning, Tyl. That's all."

Tyl patted his knee. "That'll happen when you spend all night staring at the waves, Pan." She dug a blueberry out of her bread. "Come on, we can explore the sea caves at the cove today."

She flew off, the bread falling from his knee as she bit into the juicy blueberry in her hands.

CHAPTER TWO

The Red Waistcoat

"Hit the deck!"

Cannon shot smashed through the rail above the heads of Kaylen's crew. Screams split the air. Chunks of wooden debris rained down on the hunched pirates.

"She's putting up a right fight, Captain," called Luke.

Kaylen looked to his first mate. The tree-like man in more than just stature stood at the helm, keeping the ship on course while Kaylen handled the boarding party.

"Agreed," Kaylen called back with a laugh. "They must have something awful pretty on board, aye?"

The crew joined in the laughter, the joking of their captain enough to break the tension of the coming assault. It was a merchant vessel they'd chased down. The hunt had been arduous. They'd followed the sleek, dark green ship after it had snuck away from the mainland bay in the middle of the night.

Kaylen's crew of oddities had been the only reason they hadn't lost the other ship in those first few dark hours. Luke wasn't the only one with fae blood in his veins.

Kaylen shifted his attention to the small woman in the crow's nest. "Numbers still in our favor, El?"

He got a yelp of confirmation from above, followed by another cheer from the crew.

"Six seconds, Kay!" Luke called.

Kaylen drew his cutlass with his right hand, the other pulling a dagger from his boot. "Ready, crew," he bellowed.

The seconds seemed to slow.

Kaylen pressed his fingers to the violet amulet around his neck. It wasn't meant for luck, but he'd take any it had to give regardless.

He leaned forward, his breath held. It happened every time. The brief moments before the ships collided stretched out ahead of him... the sea churning below... the thick hull braced from within... the seconds ticking... and then.

A mighty crash as the hulls collided. Wood splintered, men shouted, and Kaylen leapt.

His boots landed with a sharp thud on the deck of the other ship. He straightened, brushed a wisp of his dark hair out of his face, and strode forward with his chin high.

Half his crew followed. The others worked to secure the ships together so the merchant ship couldn't escape.

The green of the deck and the colors flown above proclaimed this hunk of wood belonged to one of the main three shipping companies running goods from the large mainland continent to the smattering of islands across the sea.

What Kaylen expected to find in the hull would mean one of two things. Either the captain of the ship was trying to earn on the side, or the company was going to have a lot of explaining to do.

Not that any of that mattered in the moment. Kaylen's focus was on the men coming toward him.

They knew who he was. Knew it from the red of his coat, the gold paint detailing his ship, and the black colors flying from the mast.

Pirates were dangerous. Kaylen and his crew... they were something else.

His lips split into a grin as the first two men charged. He ducked, weaved, parried. Knocked the blade from one. Sent the other spinning into the rail with a grunt of pain.

The others came at him with less gumption. Fear flickered in their gazes. Some had cheeks wet with tears.

Kaylen laid them low, avoiding death where possible, but not slowing his blade. Around him, his crew did the same. Those who surrendered were spared—for now.

Mere moments after the attack, the merchant ship was won. Its crew lay dead or tied to the mast. Two of Kaylen's crew held the captain in place at the helm.

Kaylen stared out at it all with a heavy weight on his chest.

It was progress, catching these last dregs of the business his father had created. Catching them and delivering the same justice he'd given the man himself only ten years prior.

A decade since Captain James Hook had unwillingly passed his blood-red waistcoat onto his son.

A decade, yet the remains of his empire still sailed through the cracks.

Someone's hand landed on Kaylen's arm, and he jerked his head. Only Zeyda, a pale woman with orc blood somewhere in her northern lineage. She met his gaze with nearly white eyes and cocked her head.

"Everything all right, Cap?" The traces of her northern accent were barely present after a few months at sea.

He nodded. "Let's get below and confirm our suspicions." His lip curled as he looked up at the captain of the merchant ship. "Then we'll deal with this lot."

Zeyda bowed her head and strode toward the storage grate that led below deck. As thick as she was, people still didn't expect the strength she wielded. Her fingers wrapped around the grate and, without waiting for someone to find the key, she ripped the thing from its hinges.

Kaylen's crew roared their approval.

Zeyda's nearly translucent cheeks went pink. Her shyness over the use of her strength faded with each cheer of support from the crew. She set the grate against the secondary mast.

Kaylen made to move below deck when a voice carried across the end of the cheers.

"You've got no rights here, Kaylen," the merchant captain called. "Pirates can't arrest regular folk. Where would you take us, huh? Back to the mainland? They'll chase you from the docks soon as we tell them what you are. Or, better yet, they'll hang the lot of you."

Kaylen's back was to the man, and so he did not mind being unable to keep the vicious sneer from his face. He inhaled, straightened the lapel of his blood red jacket, and carried on down the stairs.

"Is he right?" Zeyda whispered as she followed him. "What'll we do with 'em if we can't take 'em in?"

"He's not right," Kaylen said. He reached for a dangling lantern, its wick cold and dry. "Flint."

Zeyda obliged, lighting the lamp as the two of them continued into the belly of the boat. Light filtered through portholes, but it was almost entirely obscured on one side by Kaylen's ship.

"Even if we couldn't take them to a *respectable* port," Kaylen murmured as his boots found purchase at the bottom of the stairs. "We could take them back to the towns they stole from. The people there would handle it."

"Is that what we'll do?" Zeyda asked, peering through the darkness.

The storage area was a bit ahead, past a few rows of hammocks that reeked of sweat and lemons.

Kaylen picked up his pace. He didn't like the dark. The way it pushed in on him, suffocating and tight. He held the lamp higher, but it did little to spread the light.

A second later, they reached what they sought.

Zeyda gasped.

Kaylen exhaled a furious breath.

"No," he said, his jaw tight. "That's not what we'll do."

CHAPTER THREE

Fae Blood

T he youngest of the children was maybe five or six. The oldest, about ten.

The same age Kaylen had been when he'd realized what his pirate of a father truly traded in.

It hadn't been gold.

"Get them out," he said to Zeyda.

She hurried to the keys dangling from a hook a few feet away. Within a moment, the cage was open and the half-dozen children within were stepping out on shaky legs.

"Were there more of you?" Kaylen asked the oldest looking boy. "Did they do any sort of drop or trade?"

He shook his head, fluffy black curls dropping across his face.

Kaylen exhaled a sigh of relief. "And you're all from the same village?"

"Yes, sir." The boy's voice was hoarse and scratched.

Kaylen worked to block the mental image of the children screaming for their mothers from his head. He reached a gentle hand to take the boy's elbow. The two started up the stairs, the others trailing behind with Zeyda.

"Not far from the port, sir," the boy said. "It were only a short while in the carriage before we was put on the ship."

"Good. Won't be hard to get you back home then."

One of the little ones stepped timidly onto the deck and stared up at the various crew around her. Kaylen's mates weren't exactly a normal looking bunch. But the sight of them didn't seem to deter her.

She looked at Kaylen with wide eyes. The evidence of her bloodline was minimal, only the golden ring around her irises suggested she was the descendant of some kind of fae creature. "We're going home?"

"Aye," he said, the corner of his mouth twitching up into a half-smile. "Home by end of day tomorrow, if the wind is feeling kind."

"She is, Captain," Luke confirmed. The helmsman had left the wheel in the hands of a greener crewmember while the ships were latched together. "But we oughta be goin' soon."

Kaylen nodded. He pointed to three of his crew. "You lot get the children stowed away safe. The rest of yeh–" he turned, meeting the eye of the merchant captain who thought it was a good idea to trade human lives–"gut this boat."

They left the green ship with naught but luck to guide their way. Kaylen's crew had taken every scrap of valuable goods–they were still pirates, after all–and had dismantled the sails and rigging.

With luck, another ship would stumble across them and feel merciful. Unlikely, given the message Luke had pressed into the wood on either side of the ship. The word *Slavers* hadn't taken him more than a few minutes to grow, moss splintering out of the wood as his rare brand of magic marked the ship.

Without luck... it didn't take long for sailors to succumb to dehydration on the ocean. Add in the number of sirens known to search for drifting ships. It wasn't likely those *merchants* would ever be seen again.

"Two days to the mainland." Zeyda walked up beside Kaylen, her heavy footfalls alerting him before she arrived. "What after that, Captain?"

Kaylen spread his arms in a long stretch. He'd stowed his waistcoat away in his quarters. It had served its purpose, and now he was comfortable in the late afternoon heat with just the tunic on his back. "Good question."

There'd been no injuries during the taking of the ship, which meant a stop at the healer they frequented was unnecessary.

They did have a plethora of goods in need of unloading. Some they could trade with reputable merchants, but most they'd need to take to one of the pirate ports found in the islands to the west.

His heart gave a jolt, and he turned to look toward the slowly setting sun. One of those islands had been calling to him for a while.

"We could head to the Isles," Luke said from where he was wiping the remains of thick green moss from his bark-like fingers. His gruff voice matched the dark streaks of wood that crossed his caramel complexion. Though just as old as Kaylen, Luke's lines of bark aged him well past their twenty-four years.

Kaylen shot his first mate a sharp look, but Luke maintained an innocent expression.

"That'd be wise," Kaylen agreed, trying not to sound overly eager. "Plenty of ports to trade in."

"Aye," Luke agreed. "And Zeyda's yet to see Never Land."

Heat poured into Kaylen's cheeks. He waved a hand, as though to cover his blush. "That's not a bad idea, Luke."

"And I'm sure I was the first one to think of it," the tree-like man said with a wicked grin. "Yeh weren't thinkin' about it from the second those goods started loading onto the ship."

Kaylen squinted at his friend, but the warmth in his chest and cheeks couldn't be denied. "It'll be good to do some trading with the Never Landers." He looked at Zeyda. "They don't use gold. But they always have some interesting magical items we can barter for."

Her brow furrowed as she glanced from captain to first mate. "Isn't the island called Never Land because it's forbidden to humans?"

Kaylen shrugged. "That won't be a problem."

Luke chuckled and explained, "We don't go onto the island, Zeyda. You're right. It's forbidden. Our contacts there come to us."

"Huh."

Kaylen chuckled. "You'll see. Wouldn't want to spoil the surprise for yeh."

Luke rolled his eyes and clapped a hand on Kaylen's shoulder. "First, we deposit the children with their families."

"Aye," Kaylen agreed. He exhaled a tight breath, the thrill at the prospect of going back to Never Land leaving him quickly. His gaze flickered back the way they'd come, thoughts returning to the ship they'd gutted and left for dead. "I don't know how so many slipped through our grasp."

His friend nodded. "I've been wonderin' the same. It's been over a decade since we took the old man down. His ilk should be long gone."

A shiver ran down Kaylen's spine. He recalled, in a brief flash of memory, the scream of fury his father had uttered when he'd found out Kaylen had betrayed him.

It had been nothing compared to the cries of the children their ship had once stolen away from their families.

Children with any ounce of fae blood James Hook could find.

Luke had been one of them. Almost as old as Kaylen, but locked in the hold below, not working as cabin boy to the captain.

How might Kaylen's life have changed if he'd not befriended Luke then? If he'd not felt that stirring deep in his gut that told him how utterly *wrong* his father was?

If he hadn't watched a flying boy slice Captain James's hand from his arm and learned then and there that his father wasn't untouchable.

He could be hurt.

He could be stopped.

He could be killed.

"Hey." Luke gave Kaylen's shoulder a gentle shake. "We'll get them, Kay. We're not stopping 'til every one of those bastards is dealt with."

A few of the crew nearby made sounds of confirmation. Most of them had been there that day ten years ago. Most had spent their later teen years and young adult life serving under Captain Kaylen.

He hadn't asked for the title. But he'd been the only one left who knew how to work a ship. Then, by the time they'd worked out surviving enough to consider doing more, the routine had felt natural. He *was* their captain. They were his crew.

Kaylen flashed his friend a grateful smile. "All right, enough jabber. Let's ride this wind to the mainland and get these little ones home."

The crew sprang into action. A young woman with flaming red hair and sharp, talon-like nails hurried the children below deck. Not to the hold, which looked too similar to the merchant ship to be any kind of comfort. She'd get them settled into hammocks in the crew quarters.

The others manned the ship, getting them up to speed and cutting across the water within minutes.

Kaylen inhaled the sea air, the salty scent grounding him as he took the helm. Another slaver ship brought low.

Another corrupted piece of his soul made clean.

He stared out at the ocean, watching the deep water move. He breathed in another steadying breath, his heart heavy despite the promising view of the horizon.

Chapter Four

Muffins

Clara cocked her little head at Tyl, and the fairy wondered, not for the first time, how long it would take for the child to learn to crack an egg without dumping half the shells into the bowl.

One would think her pixie ancestry might have given her more grace than a regular mortal, but it seemed all the Lost Ones of that age were as clumsy as their boring human counterparts.

"The recipe calls for three eggs, girl." Tyl perched on the edge of the bowl, reaching in with her hands and plucking the grey and green speckled shells from the batter. "Not three eggs and their shells. You won't be allowed to help with the baking if you can't get that sorted."

The girl, a wide-eyed thing who had only been on the island for a few months... or was it weeks? Tyl couldn't remember. It had been longer than a day or two, at least. The girl blinked down at Tyl. Her eyes grew wet.

"No, no, no," Tyl said, the first 'no' stern and the last almost a plea. "I wasn't mean about it, Clara. Please don't cry. Ohhh." She sighed as the girl's blonde curls shook back and forth with her sobs.

"Hey."

Both Tyl and Clara jumped, turning to the ivy-framed archway as Pan walked in and planted his hands on his hips.

He looked from the fairy to the child, who was sniffling. "Tyl..."

"I didn't do *anything*," Tyl complained. "We can't have shells in the batter. It can't be that hard to crack the eggs. You do it all the time."

Pan rubbed the bridge of his nose. "I'm not five, Tyl." He bent to one knee, grinned at Clara, and said in a conspiratorial voice, "Is the fairy being mean again?"

The girl shot a glance at Tyl.

Deflated, Tyl dropped the shells onto the counter and crossed her arms over her chest. She leaned on one leg, tapping her toe on the side of the bowl where she still balanced.

Frustration, annoyance, and remorse were battling it out in her mind and, as there was not room for all three, the jumbled mess only added to the annoyance.

"I didn't mean to mess it up," Clara sniffed.

"I know." Pan stood and lifted the child, holding her on his hip.

Tyl settled on remorse and annoyance, deciding in the moment that the two could go hand in hand if she really worked at it.

She wiped her hands on the minuscule pink apron around her waist. The one, she remembered begrudgingly as remorse took the lead, that Clara had cut out of her sleeping gown just after she'd been found.

The Lost Ones weren't new to Tyl by any means. Most were children who'd been lost and somehow managed to find Never Land. The running theory was that they'd been abandoned due to some odd fae attribute or another. *How* they ended up on Never Land was a question Tyl had considered a few times over the years, but had never dug into as something else always caught her attention and fully distracted her.

They never stayed too long. A short while as they grew taller and wider and smarter, then when they'd reached the cusp of adulthood—if not before—Pan would send them on their way with one of the few merchant vessels that occasionally stopped in the bay.

Pan had been the first, Tyl the one to find him.

She blinked as the remorse touched nostalgia. When had he stopped being as small as Clara?

Her lips turned down in a half pout, half frown as she pondered the speed with which he'd grown. It was lucky she knew of the spring. Lucky she'd watched the queen's guards enough times to know when she could sneak him there. Lucky the queen had no notion of the growth speed of humans. And, perhaps luckiest of all, that none of the fairies in the Hollow had ever shown an ounce of desire to visit the great oak tree.

Fairies kept to the northern part of the island, not wanting to venture into the sliver of dangerous land to the south. As such, they'd not found any issue with how many children appeared and disappeared over time.

Another of Tyl's many successful tricks. Even if this one meant eggshells in the muffin batter.

Tyl's head tipped to the side as she surveyed Pan and Clara. How long would this little one stay with them? She'd long learned not to get too attached. Pan was the only one to stay. Not only because she loved him the most, but also because the queen had long since destroyed the spring.

Fairies were the only *immortal* beings on Never Land. When the discovery had been made that the spring granted that rare gift to any who drank from it, she'd had it buried in stone.

"I got the shells out," Tyl said as a form of repentance for making the child cry. "Come, Clara, let's finish the muffins."

Pan shot Tyl a twisted grin as the girl scurried back to the stump she'd stood on to reach the table.

Clara wiped her nose with the back of her arm, grabbed a bowl of blueberries, and dumped them into the not-yet-incorporated egg mixture.

"Well." Tyl planted her hands on her hips, wrestling down another burst of frustration as Pan broke into laughter. "All right, then."

Chapter Five

Big Emotions

When the muffins were done, Tyl and Pan left the Oak for their usual morning adventures. Berries needed picking, fish needed catching, and mischief needed doing.

Tyl rode Pan's shoulder as he walked along the mossy path that led from the multi-level tree-house to the edge of the clearing. Trees surrounded them. The winding branches, dripping with ivy and floral stems twisting up their trunks, grew thicker on the side of the path leading into the forest and thinner on the side that led to the little cove.

There was another cove, larger but blocked by massive stones that jutted from the water and warned away ships. It was on the northeastern side of the island. The one they headed to now was small, with a pale sandy beach, gentle lapping waves, and only the occasional sea monster trying to eat anyone who got too close.

Not that such things stopped Pan and Tyl from splashing in the water whenever they felt like it. If anything, Tyl often hoped for a new beast of some kind so they could practice their fighting. Her little blade didn't do nearly as much damage as Pan's, but she did get a chance to practice battle magic when there was a crawly from the deep trying to sneak onto the island to eat the fae folk.

"What's the plan today, Pan?" she asked, stretching her neck. The chill morning air caressed her gossamer wings as she unfurled and extended them.

Pan darted a side-long glance her way and, with the full breadth of their history together, the hairs on the back of her neck stood on end. Suspicion collided with the excitement of promised adventure, and she flew from his shoulder.

She whirled around, facing him a foot from his nose. "Pan?" Her tiny voice carried an accusatory question.

Pan sighed and stepped around her. He continued down the path to where the woods met the thick round rocks at the top of the beach. "I got a raven a few nights ago. Kaylen'll be here today or tomorrow, depending on the winds."

Tyl's eyes went wide. She clenched her hands into fists, nails digging into her palm. Shooting a look back at the Oak brought a twinge of sadness to her heart despite the anger running rampant through her veins.

"Care to explain why you didn't *tell* me?" she snapped, fluttering along beside him as he jumped and deftly flew over the rocks before dropping until his feet found the sand.

Pan planted his hands on his hips, cocking his head and raising an eyebrow. "Last time you tried to stab him."

She glowered. "Last time he called me a pixie. I'm not a pixie."

Pan's mischievous smile cooled the heat of her temper a bit. "Oh Tyl, you know pirates and mainlanders don't know the first thing about the tiny folk. You can't hold that against them."

"I can, and I will." Tyl crossed her arms, pinching her eyebrows together to keep the furrow in her brow–despite her internal acknowledgement that his words were correct.

Of course the pirate didn't know the difference. A mainlander would be even more clueless about the goings-on of fae folk. Still, she didn't trust the man. Not even a little.

Pan plunked down in the sand, his legs stretched out ahead of him and an easy smile on his face. "You don't have to like him, but he'll have supplies we need. Besides, we're running out of room in the Oak. Some of the Lost Ones are getting old enough to move on."

Heat flared again and, though his words were nothing but true, Tyl was once again consumed by anger. This time tinged just a little with fear.

"I don't understand why you think we can trust him, Pan." Tyl hovered in front of him. "Not after what he's done."

Pan's smile evaporated. "That's not fair, Tyl, and you know it. He was a child."

"So?" She lowered, and Pan's knee came up automatically for her to rest on. "The children at the Oak know better."

"It's not always about knowing better," Pan said. "You get confused sometimes, Tyl, because I look young still, but I'm actually not. Children, actual children, don't get a say in what happens to them. In where they go, or what they do, or who they're with. They get dragged around by adults until they're old enough to make their own way."

"You made your own way long before I took you to the fountain," Tyl grumbled.

Pan laughed. The sound mingled with the lapping of the gentle waves on the soft shore.

He leaned back on his hands, pointing his face to the sky and letting the light shine down on his already sun-kissed skin. "Don't you remember when you first found me, Tyl? The wee boy washed up on the shore. You had to magic me still so I wouldn't go grabbing poisonous jelly-fish."

The fire in her was dying, slowly extinguished by his logical words and calming tone. Yet her heart thudded hard inside her chest. Her mind flashed to the race. To Pan's hesitation and the way he looked talking about *change*.

She rolled her eyes. "Say what you will, but he's a slaver, Pan. Reformed or not, we can't trust him."

Pan straightened. He narrowed a calculated gaze on her, his smile missing again. In a soft voice, almost too low, he said, "It wasn't his choice to be on that ship, Tyl. Nor was it within his power to leave."

She buzzed up from his knee, arms spread wide as she glared at him. "He tried to kill you!"

Pan shook his head. "He was *defending* himself. You know that."

Tyl threw up her arms in frustration. "Not that he needed to," she said with a sneer. "You defend him plenty enough for the both of you."

Pan sighed, and the exasperation in his expression only served to stoke her anger. "I'm not asking you to like him, Tyl. But we *do* have to trust him." He looked back toward the Oak. In a gesture far too like a grown-up for Tyl's taste, he rubbed a hand across his face, leaving a streak of sand on his cheek. "He's the only way to get them safely off the island."

She flew in a circle, burning some of the heat out of her chest as little sparks of fairy dust glittered in her wake. "I could... I could teach them to fly. Then we'd go on mainland adventures again."

His face darkened. "No. Not again, Tyl. We can't meddle in people's lives like that."

She flushed but waved away his words with a grunt. "Well, still. I could teach them and we'd–"

"Tyl."

She spun around, refusing to look at him.

"You know why we can't do that. The queen gave you an allowance to teach *me*. You can't teach *everyone* to fly.

It would lead to questions. If she found out you took me to the spring..."

They both paused, the frustration between them frozen for a few brief seconds as the dread of what would happen if the fairy queen discovered what Tyl had done all those years ago overwhelmed them both.

Tyl snapped out of the fear first. She faced Pan, flying closer to his face and looking him in the eye. "I don't care, Pan. He's a pirate, and I don't trust him."

Pan opened his mouth, but she soared upwards. Up, up, up, and away into the sky, letting the wind lift her glittering wings. The rest of her anger burned out, fairy dust sprinkling the air behind her as she headed, for the first time in far too long, to the Hollow.

CHAPTER SIX

The Hollow

Tyl flew through the trees until the anger was out of her body and the fairy dust behind her had faded. When it was gone, she was left with an annoying feeling of emptiness.

Which was extra annoying because that empty feeling wasn't there when she had more than one emotion swirling up inside her at a time. She clung to the annoyance as she soared over the forest.

The trees below grew taller, their dense green at odds with the vibrant pastels of spring erupting from every inch of spare room.

Ahead of her, rising up like a turret above the green canopy, was the Hollow.

It towered high enough to be spotted from miles out to sea. The top, thickest with leaves, was where most of fairie-kind lived. Halfmoon mushroom roofs jutted from the bark, overhangs for the little houses carved into the wood. Dangling houses woven together from ivy and vine hung from the sturdy branches.

The tree itself was massive. Magic during the early years of its life had allowed it to grow thick but hollow, with a grand hall at the base and curling stairs leading up to the higher branches. The hall itself had been created large enough for the various human and fae kings and queens who had once come to hold court with the fairy queen to comfortably visit.

That had been long before Tyl's time. The grand rooms stretching on either side of the hall–for the visitors who couldn't fly and were likely too heavy for branches–had been transformed into barracks for the queen's guard, storage for her many treasures, and prison for those foolish enough to cross her.

Tyl glided down, annoyance still front and center as she flitted through the immensely tall arch that led into the queen's hall.

Plenty of fae folk visited the Hollow, though fairies were the ones who called it home. The front entrance was filled with wares. Pixies traded their leatherwork, textiles, and rare gems. Tree-folk offered runes grown into small stones and staffs of protection. Fairies carted fruits, baked goods, and other various foods.

The thriving market called Tyl's attention only for a brief moment. Usually, she'd mark a visit to the Hollow by bringing Pan a small gift. But this had been an unanticipated visit, and she'd brought nothing to trade. Besides, a tiny part of her was still mad at him.

She flew over the heads of the merchants with grumbling in her belly. She needed to find Mira. Her friend would have something to quell her hunger.

Mighty and grand as the Hollow was, Tyl couldn't help the disappointment that sprouted up alongside her annoyance at the sight of even more stonework in the bustling hall.

Where soft moss had once been the feeling underfoot, now it was off-white stone. The slabs had been cut with magic, the stones pulled from the beaches around the island–though not the ones on the southern end. It had taken the fairy court a long while to cover the ground floor of the Hollow.

Tyl had, fortunately, been busy with Pan around that time. When she'd finally returned from one of their longer adventures, the Hollow hadn't been what she remembered.

Though she hadn't been gone long this time, still more had been changed.

The queen's throne sat at the far end of the hall. It was empty at the moment, the queen far too busy to simply sit and watch the fairies hurrying about on their daily business. The throne, too, was stone. A shiny black with jagged points at the tip of the high-backed chair. Wide benches of grey stone sat on either side, a resting place for the more important members of her court.

Even without the queen present, her fairy guards hovered at the front of the dais, gazes locked forward. They were the rare ones of the flying folk, having traded leaf and cloth for metal. Silver armor hung from their shoulders, cuffed their forearms, and covered their feet. Each held a spear at their side.

The pressing disappointment amplified as Tyl caught sight of the stairs. Winding wooden steps had been meticulously grown—magic doing what nature alone could not. They were dark, the russet shade of thick bark, and circled the interior of the Hollow. Though far too fairie-sized for large visitors, the stairs were how pre-winged fairies reached the higher branches. They were how a fairy with a broken wing reached the infirmary. They carried a history in them... a story of a time before wings, when magic was just beginning for fairie-kind.

Tyl floated in a circle, her lips parted in a dismayed expression. The first several dozen bark steps had been replaced. Slivers of more grey stone were where the wood once grew, pressed into the interior trunk of the Hollow.

Her disappointment grew to anger once again as she noted the thin drips of sap curling down the smooth wood of the trunk.

Tyl clenched her hands, pressing her lips together to avoid a shout that would undeniably call attention to herself. She hadn't come for attention. She'd come to find a friend who *wasn't* trying to replace her with a pirate.

The thought landed so heavy on her chest she sank a full several inches. It was when her toes brushed the hard ground that she realized she'd stopped hovering.

"Tyl?"

She whirled.

A tree-folk stood just past the market at the entrance of the hall. His thick face was bearded with brown moss, the features enhanced and exaggerated by the way his bark-like skin grew with age.

"Finch," she said with a grin.

Her feet left the cold stone floor, wings lifting and carrying her to her old friend and instructor. She hovered a few feet off the ground to meet his eye. Though most stood not as tall as the average human, tree-folk were still considerably larger than fairies.

She met his sage green eyes, noting less twinkle in them now than the last time they'd crossed paths. "How are you? I haven't seen you in some time."

"Some time, indeed," he said with a creaky smile.

Finch took a hesitant step into the hall, wincing as his bare feet touched the stone.

"Everything all right?" Tyl asked, floating back to keep in step with him.

He nodded, patting his hip with a gnarled hand. "Just getting up there in years, Tyl. You hit a hundred and the next fifty seem to fly by. These new floors don't help any."

A guard hovering nearby grunted, and Finch waved a hand.

"Pay no mind to my old grumbles," he said with a grimace. "How are you these days, Tyl?"

Tyl's brow furrowed. Her gaze fixed for a moment on the fairy guard. She took a second to look around again, focused on the people rather than the place, and realized there were nearly a dozen of the metal-clad figures just on the ground level of the Hollow.

"I..." she hesitated, distracted. "Uh, I'm well, Finch. How are you? What brings you to the Hollow?"

He sighed, running a hand across his dark mossy beard. "The queen sent a missive. There is an announcement to be made this afternoon." He leaned in with a wink. "Rumblings suggest it's about the summer solstice festival. Bigger than ever this year." His eyes squeezed together with his wide grin. "What brings you down to the hall? Shouldn't you be up in the branches enjoying the fresh air?" He chuckled. "Or off causing trouble with that human of yours?"

Tyl laughed. "Don't worry, we still do plenty of that. I'm looking for Mira is all."

He bobbed his head. "I do believe the spring fairies are out doing what they do best this time of year."

Tyl's eyes went wide and she slapped a palm to her forehead. A rush of chagrin, and then excitement, shot through her. "Of course! Thanks, Finch. I'll see you around."

"Be sure to get back for the announcement, Tyl. I don't want to see you or Mira getting in any trouble."

She only heard half the goodbye that followed his very instructor-like comment before she was gone, flitting through the air like a dandelion seed in the wind.

CHAPTER SEVEN

Strawberry Fairy

The excitement mingled with a softer emotion as she left the Hollow, weaving up and down and around other fairies doing the same, and headed even further north.

There was a valley between the Hollow and the cove at the northern tip of the island. It was where spring had begun on the island for as long as anyone could remember.

Staying low and skimming the treetops, gladness found a home beside excitement as Tyl flew.

A spot of pink was visible amongst the pale green strands of grass at the edge of the wide valley. Tyl grinned.

"Mira," she called, soaring down and landing beside an only-slightly-taller fairy with brilliant pink hair the color of a butterfly bush in full bloom and freckles dotting her pale complexion.

Her friend of however many years the two had been alive looked up from her work. A wide smile split her face and she pulled a hand from the soil, waving it up at Tyl.

The valley was empty of trees at the moment. Perhaps a pox or fungus had required their removal. Tyl wasn't sure the specifics of it–court workings were never anything she had an interest in–but Mira was still doing her job of filling the valley with spring flowers.

A job, Tyl remembered for the briefest of moments, that she was technically supposed to be doing as well. She brushed the thought aside. There were plenty of spring fairies handling spring in the north. She did plenty of growing by the Oak to compensate for shirking her duties here.

Tyl darted downward, coming to land beside Mira with a smile to rival her friend's. "Looks great. You've outdone yourself this year."

Mira raised a pink eyebrow, then turned to look out at the rolling grassy hills before them.

The valley was a much beloved place amongst the fairy court. Tyl and Mira had been infants no larger than Pan's thumb playing under the shade of the trees that had once dotted the hillsides. Before their wings had come in, they'd spent their days exploring every inch of what had once seemed a vast space.

It had gotten smaller, Tyl thought. Long before Pan came along, she'd outgrown the valley. And now... Her eyes watered. She stooped, cupping a flower bud with her palm and gently feeding magic into the thing.

It grew, reaching the height of her shoulder before blooming into a beautiful yellow bell-shaped flower.

"Glad to see you haven't *actually* forgotten how to do a fairy's job," Mira muttered, the words just loud enough for Tyl to hear.

They were relatively alone. Other flower fairies dotted the valley, bringing color to life. Even more flitted about in the woods, caring for the trees and tending to the moss and mushrooms and wild things that grew in dark, damp ground.

Many worked with the tree-folk, ensuring their lands were healthy. And a contingent served with the pixies as well, though they had fewer hands-on tasks.

Tyl's dark cheeks warmed, but the remark was fair enough. She'd been gone for some time. Not that it particularly mattered. There were plenty of fairies to help the flowers grow.

Tyl didn't respond to Mira's jab. Instead, she walked a slow circle around her friend, touching the dirt here and there, cupping flowers and helping them bloom in time to catch the sun's late morning rays.

When she'd completed the area Mira had been working on, she turned to find the pink-haired fairy looking disgruntled.

"What?" she asked. A fullness in her heart sang at the use of magic, even with the drain she felt.

Mira shook her head. "You make it impossible to be mad at you."

Tyl cackled. "Untrue. But thank you." She strode to her friend, looping her arm and walking with her to the next patch of dirt that needed greenery.

It wasn't far, but her breath caught when they arrived. The dry patch wasn't what she'd thought, a simple gap in the grass. For one, it was larger than she'd assumed from a distance. It was also surrounding a stump.

She detached from Mira and flew to the thing, her hand pressing the thin rings that marked the tree's now-ended life. Pain sparked, like a shock of lightning from the stump to her hand as she pushed her skin into the wood. Her magic caressed the bark, reading the once-living thing as though it were a book. It hadn't been sick. Tears burned at the inside corners of her eyes.

Trees fell. They fell and died. Everything died, eventually. Even fairies, though their lives wouldn't end on their own.

This tree had been slain. The cut was too clean. It hadn't fallen on its own.

"What's this?" Tyl asked, turning to look at Mira. "It wasn't sick?"

Her friend sighed. "It must have been. There may be some kind of illness spreading. The tree fairies have been all in a tither."

"I don't feel any illness. Couldn't the queen–" Tyl stopped herself, twisting her lips to the side in a grimace. "Wouldn't one of the more powerful of the court be able to do something about it? Cutting it…"

She winced, putting her hand once more on the stump and feeling the residual surge of pain. She closed her eyes and consumed the feeling. It overflowed in her and poured out, tears of glittering dust dripping from her cheeks.

She pulled away, looking at Mira. "This seems extreme."

Mira glanced furtively in the direction of the Hollow. "I'm sure they had a reason, Tyl. Let's get it ready and sow the ground."

Tyl wiped her eyes, tracks of golden liquid staining her clothes where she dried her fingers. Then the two of them got to work.

Their magic seeped into the trunk of the once-tree, turning the hard wood into a soft place where critters might find a home. When that had been done, they sowed the ground with seeds Mira carried in a pouch at her waist. Tyl had left hers at the Oak, not having planned on actually visiting the Hollow that day.

"I worry about you, you know?" Mira said as the two of them dug into the ground. "Being gone so often."

Tyl used her magic to drift a few strawberry seeds into the holes, then nudged the dirt back on top with her bare feet. "I'm not gone *that* much, Mira."

Her friend raised both eyebrows in an incredulous stare.

Tyl stuck out her tongue. "I'm not."

"How many nights have you spent at the Hollow this month?" Mira demanded gently, she pulled another handful of seeds and scattered them across the ground. With her hands out, palms flat, she shook them. The dirt shook as well, the seeds drifting down and becoming layered by the soft soil.

"I..." Tyl frowned, trying to remember. Mira had always been better at keeping track of the passage of time than she had. It was to do with being a seasonal fairy. Tyl was a different sort. One of the kind that could use their magic for a variety of needs.

Tyl kicked a clump of dirt. "I don't know. It's hard to sleep there anymore."

Mira glanced toward the massive tree.

Tyl continued. "You know I can't stand all the stone they've been putting in. It's too cold. Freezes my wings, Mira. And then I can't sleep at all."

Her friend sighed. "Yeah. Freezes mine, too. The smoother the floors and walls, the colder it gets."

"Exactly." Tyl shook her head. "I prefer the Oak." The corner of her mouth crooked up in a conspiratorial grin. "You could join me there, you know. Come play with the Lost Ones, have some mortal food, sleep under the stars again..."

She looked up at the end of her words, gaze drawn to the top branches of the Hollow.

As younglings, she and Mira had enjoyed their time in the valley, sleeping in the flowers, as was custom. When they'd both sprouted wings, they'd been given homes above.

Having to leave the dirt she loved so much might have been the first time Tyl had felt the frustration that so eagerly coursed through her veins. It certainly wasn't the last.

"I can see the stars just fine from my window, Tyl," Mira said with a sigh. She dusted her hands off on the pale purple petals that made up her skirt. With a stern look at the plants they'd just brought to sunlight, she took hold of Tyl's upper arm and lifted into the air.

Tyl followed her lead, letting the pink fairy bring her into the shade of the nearby edge of the forest.

They landed among the moss and leaves, the ground still damp from the unseasonably late winter storm they'd gotten recently. Mira sat on the edge of a saddle mushroom growing from a branch that had fallen sometime during the winter.

The scent of the wet earth, the rich green moss, and the decomposing leaves made Tyl's nose itch. She wiggled her upper lip to rid herself of the itch then joined Mira on the mushroom.

Tyl leaned forward and planted her elbows on her knees as she frowned over at her friend's uncharacteristic lack of bubbly joy. "What's wrong, Mira?"

Mira sighed, her fingers drifting to her hair and twisting the strands of pink together into a braid. "I'm worried about you."

Tyl straightened. "Worried?"

"Worried," Mira said again, her words getting quieter like they always did when she was battling more than one emotion at a time. "You've been gone from the Hollow so much lately, you haven't seen the things happening here."

"I don't need to *see* fairies ruining the Hollow with all that ugly stone, Mira."

"Shh," her friend snapped.

Tyl blinked, startled.

"You can't say such things anymore, Tyl. By the roots down deep, have you *really* been paying so little attention?"

A twinge of hurt spiked through Tyl's chest. "I... I pay attention," she said, her usually sturdy voice frustratingly meek. She sniffed and shot a glare at Mira. "You know I've never cared about court politics, Mira. I prefer–"

"I know, I know," Mira interrupted. "You prefer adventures to the boring life we live at the Hollow. But things are getting dangerous, Tyl. You can't say things like you do."

"Things like what?"

Mira waved her arms, her cheeks going pink as she spoke in an anxious, quiet voice. "Like hating the stone floors. Like the cutting of the trees. The *queen* is the one making those changes. You can't *say* she's wrong like that."

"Why in the roots *not*? She can't hear me."

Mira's movement was too fast for Tyl to track until her friend was directly in front of her face. Her body was tilted, nose inch to inch with Tyl's, pale hands cupping Tyl's rich, sepia cheeks.

"You *cannot* say things like that, Tyl." Mira's voice got lower still, nearly a whisper, as though she was mouthing the words.

And Tyl realized she was. She was mouthing the words, and letting her hands carry the sound to Tyl's ears with magic.

"She's got eyes everywhere now, Tyl. She's watching the forest. Every territory, even as far south as the Oak. I don't understand it. Don't know all of what's going on. But you must be careful. Because you're my friend, and I love you, and I don't want anything bad to happen to you."

Tyl sat silent and still for a long moment, looking into her friend's lavender eyes and reading the whirling sea of fear and anxiety there. Slowly, as though stepping through a glade without wanting to startle a fawn, she nodded.

Then, just as slow, she reached up and placed her palm on Mira's freckly cheek. *"You said as far as the Oak... is she watching the Lost Ones?"*

Mira nodded.

Tyl's fingers went to her lips as she fought the rising tide of worry within. There was no reason to think the queen would find anything amiss at the Oak. The Lost Ones were small, even the oldest would still be children to fairy eyes.

And Pan... Tyl had gotten special permission from the queen for Pan. Permission to keep the boy safe on the island while he was not yet a man.

"And he isn't," Tyl murmured, her voice barely a whisper.

Mira still hovered in front of her, hands now wringing together at her chest. "Tyl?"

"I understand," Tyl said. "We'll be... we'll be careful, Mira. It'll all be all right. Pan is a child still. He's allowed here by the old laws."

Mira sniffed, golden tears now running down her cheeks. "I don't know if the old laws will be enough anymore, Tyl. It's all changing so fast."

A low, deep horn blew from the Hollow.

"I flew into Finch coming to find you," Tyl murmured. She met Mira's eye. "The queen has some sort of announcement."

Mira nodded. "I know. I was going to come fill you in tonight if you hadn't come."

The horn blew again, and on either side of them, forest fairies soared past on their way to the great tree.

"We'd better go." Mira stood and reached out a hand.

Tyl took it, and the two of them made their way with the growing throng of fairies toward the Hollow.

Chapter Eight

Never Land

The wind favored them, and for it, Kaylen was both grateful and irritated. With an extra day on the trip to Never Land, he'd have had more time to prepare.

Not that he needed to prepare, he told himself. There was no reason to try and impress Pan. The two of them had a business relationship. Nothing more.

Pan would appreciate the items Kaylen and his crew had liberated from the merchant vessel. He might also have some Lost Ones in need of a new home. Kaylen would happily ferry the children as long as they needed, though in the past, most of them disembarked somewhere along the way in the trail of islands where Kaylen traded goods.

"Should be getting in within the hour, Captain," Luke said, clapping a hand on Kaylen's shoulder. "You want me to watch the ship while you go fix your hair?"

Kaylen blanched, fingers flying to his head where a tri-corner hat was perched. "What's wrong with my hair?"

Luke chuckled. "I'm messin', Kay. I swear, every time we visit Never Land yeh get wound like a spring."

"That," Kaylen said through gritted teeth, "is not true."

Luke shrugged. "Tell your face then. Yeh look like yer trying to chart a course in a storm."

Kaylen opened his mouth, realized both his fists were clenched, and closed it again. He inhaled, letting the crisp sea air fill his lungs. He *did* need to relax.

Over the course of the hour, Kaylen checked and double checked the rigging fixing their rowboats in place. They had two of them. Sturdy wooden things that would properly carry them into the bay where Pan would fly out to meet them.

"You cannot step foot on the sand," Kaylen told Zeyda. As the newest crew member, she had yet to visit the little island.

"Is it cursed?" the pale woman asked.

El dropped down beside them from her usual spot in the crow's nest. Her midnight black skin glistened with white freckles like little stars across her face and bare arms. She grinned, the hint of overly sharp teeth just barely visible in her smile.

She was small. Thin and angular, with slightly pointed ears and an ability to climb like no other. Pixie blood was the running theory, though, like most of the crew, she had no real notion of where she came from.

"It ain't cursed," she slapped a hand on Zeyda's back. Her thin voice matched her look, and danced with mischievous intent. "But curses ain't the only dangers to be found."

"So we're going to have to trade the goods on boats?" Zeyda's tone was incredulous.

Kaylen chuckled. "Don't worry about that right now. You'll see."

She grimaced. The crew had all silently agreed to let her experience the magic of Never Land with her own eyes first.

"I came down to tell yeh, Cap." El turned to Kaylen, looking up with her deep blue eyes. "We're here."

A trill of excitement raced down Kaylen's spine. He strode quickly, but calmly, to the bow of the ship. There, rising up ahead of them as though birthed by the horizon, was Never Land.

They approached from the east, but the direction did not matter when it came to how one spotted the fairy kingdom. No matter how one arrived at Never Land, the Hollow was the first thing they'd see.

The great tree had once been where kings and queens of old met and shared council with the fairy queen.

That had been stopped well over a hundred years ago. But rumors and legends of the place still circled the world. Ports were the most prevalent home for gossip, news, and mythos–usually in that order.

"It's too bright right now," El said, leaning close to Zeyda. "But when the sun goes down, you can see 'em flying. Their magic turns to gold light and trails behind 'em. That's what the fairy dust is, see?"

Kaylen smiled, not bothering to correct her even though he knew well enough the real reason. He'd watched Tyl bubble over with anger–or amusement, depending on which of them got in the best jab–enough times to know the dust came from too much emotion in their tiny bodies.

Almost a full moment later, the Oak became visible. The time it took accentuated the size difference between them. By the time the Oak was in view, they were close enough to see some of the details. Rope bridges and tree-houses adorned the vast tree.

Around it, and the Hollow, was all green. A vast forest that sometimes thinned to a wood but more often than not was too thick for a normal man to walk through.

Kaylen chuckled, his hand loosening on the rope he'd been holding. *Normal* wasn't the word used to describe anything about Never Land. From its shores to the creatures who lived there.

"Take us around, Luke," Kaylen called to the helm.

Luke turned the wheel, the crew adjusting sails accordingly, and the ship veered south.

"Cap," El leaned forward, hands on the rail as she stared into the distance. "There's somethin' funny."

He stepped forward, gazing out at the island. A few seconds later he raised an eyebrow at her. "I don't see anything."

She frowned. "There's somethin'… I can't put my finger on it. I'll be back."

He nodded, and she darted to the main mast. With fingers curled around the wood, El scurried up the mast to her crow's nest.

Another few seconds passed.

"Whaddya see?" Kaylen called up to her.

The ship had nearly reached where they'd have to anchor. The glimmering pale blue of the crescent shaped bay was calling to him.

"It's odd, Cap," she shouted down. "Like a thinning."

"Thinning what?"

She practically fell back to the deck. Her speed through the rigging was never tiring to watch. She hurried to his side, looking back out from the rail.

"The trees." She frowned. "Not down here so much, but to the north, where we came up on the island… it's not the same. I knew something was off. It's the trees."

"Huh." Kaylen rested his hand on the hilt of his sword. "That's…"

"Odd." El nodded.

"Wouldn't an island of immortal creatures be changing all the time?" Zeyda asked with her eyebrow up.

"Quite the opposite, actually," Kaylen said with a smile. "The changes on Never Land only come from the things that grow. The plants, the animals. The fairies and their folk… they like things just so."

El let out a barking laugh.

Kaylen grinned, his gaze turning back to the sandy beach where a lone figure stood. "Well, most of them, that is."

It was quick work getting the boats into the water. Kaylen went in one with Zeyda, El, and some of their goods. Luke followed close behind in the other with the majority of the things they'd brought to trade.

The weather continued to be on their side as they approached the beach. When the boats were about twenty yards from the shore, Kaylen held up a hand. He and Luke dropped miniature anchors into the water.

The gentle waves lapping against the sand were small, but they'd stopped far enough back to avoid tipping if the sea decided to play tricks on them.

"I don't–"

"Shh," El interrupted Zeyda. "Give it a sec."

Kaylen watched the shore, fiddling with the sleeves of his tunic and checking again that he'd brought both his dagger and his sword. His father's thick red waistcoat had been left in the cabin of his ship.

"There he is," Luke called.

The other three turned, following Luke's pointed hand.

Soaring out of the trees came a boy. A boy in the same way Kaylen was one. Old enough to be called a man, young enough to wonder if that title would ever apply.

Though, Pan was technically older than Kaylen. By how many years, he wasn't sure. The boy had stopped aging not long after he'd cut the hand from Kaylen's father.

Pan wore well loved pants that ended just past his knee. His curly brown hair was streaked with gold; the strands caught the sunlight overhead and glinted like fairy dust. His belt was busy with almost as many pouches and items as Luke's. And, as always, a thin dagger was sheathed at his side.

Kaylen had watched Pan fly a hundred times. Had seen it as a child, when Pan was a dark force of nature who scared even the captain of a slaver ship. Had seen it when he was older, and beginning to understand more of the world.

He'd seen it over and over since then. Every time they came to trade.

Kaylen blinked, shaking his head and watching as Pan dipped low, letting his fingers skate through the water and sending up a spray behind him. He'd watched Pan fly a hundred times.

It never got old.

⁂

Pan landed softly at the front of the boat. He half hovered, his feet balanced on the thin wooden edges and his fists on his hips.

"Captain Kaylen," he said in a mockingly deep tone. He puffed out his chest. "Speak quickly. What brings you to *my* island?"

Kaylen grinned up at him, a thrum of something warm bubbling up in his chest. "Your island, is it? Does that mean we have your permission to come ashore?"

Pan deflated, his expression turning glum for a brief moment. "Awww, you ruined it."

He didn't stay glum for long, however. He caught sight of Zeyda and a new smile lit up his face. "Hey, you've got new crew."

Kaylen nodded. "We do, indeed. Pan, meet Zeyda. Zeyda, meet Pan."

The woman's nearly white eyes widened even more as Pan leaned forward, letting his legs fly up behind him as he reached out a hand.

She took the outstretched hand in her much larger one and shook it.

Kaylen laughed as her strength surprised Pan.

He shook out his hand, landing again and this time sitting on the bench across from Kaylen.

"What've you got for me this time, Kay?"

Luke popped the lids of his crates, and Zeyda did the same in their boat. Textiles, spices, flour and lentils and other dry goods, candles, a handful of weapons, and even a pendant of gold wings on a thin chain just because Kaylen had thought Pan might like it.

Luke gave Kaylen a suspicious raised eyebrow when Pan pulled it from its pouch.

"Ohh, that's pretty," Pan murmured as he held the wings in his palm. "Almost as big as Tyl's."

"Where is that little troublemaker?" Kaylen asked, look-ing around.

The fairy was usually stuck to Pan's side, when she wasn't sneaking around Kaylen's ship trying to cause may-hem.

"A fairy?" Zeyda asked, her voice soft with awe.

Pan and Kaylen exchanged a grin.

"Aye, a fairy," Kaylen said. "And a tricky one, at that."

"She's busy." Pan didn't quite look up as he said it, but Kaylen didn't push the matter. "Anyway, this all looks great, Kay. I've got Lost Ones for you to take back with you. I told 'em to head this way in a bit. Figured we get unloaded first."

Kaylen nodded. "That'll work for us. You've got the usual?"

Pan's eyes glinted the way they did when he was remem-bering, or planning, a particularly good trick. "Let's make some room in one of these, and I'll show you."

They did just that. Luke climbed across to Kaylen's boat and Pan pushed the now crewless rowboat to the shore. He drove it into the sand and unloaded.

Kaylen watched for a little longer than necessary until Luke cleared his throat meaningfully.

"You know," his friend said, "You *could* ask him to come aboard the ship this time. Maybe we stay anchored for a few days. Share a meal or two..."

Kaylen glanced at his friend. Luke's expressions weren't always the easiest to read. Not with the bark-like texture covering parts of his face.

His eyes, though, they were always clear. And now they were bright with gentle encouragement.

Kaylen looked out at the shore where Pan was nearly done unloading. Then he looked down at his left hand. The hand Pan had cut off of his father when James had gone in search of the boy who could fly.

Kaylen's fingers curled into a fist. He shook his head. "No point in it, Luke."

His friend leaned in, speaking quietly as the other two on the boat pretended not to listen.

"Yeh don't hide it well, Kay, how much you care for him."

Kaylen's jaw went tight. He shook his head. "It doesn't matter how much I–" He broke off. "It wouldn't work, Luke. That's all there is to be said."

Luke looked as if he'd liked to say more, but El shot him a look, and he stayed silent. They watched the beach as Pan carried cloth sacks from the rocky shore to the boat. Once they were loaded, he tucked a few small boxes on top and shoved the boat back out. He flew, guiding the thing back to the others.

"Some of the same," he said, patting the sacks. "And some new things. There's one they're calling a pear. It grows like a tree, so it'll be a few years before the fruit comes without magic. But they're amazing, Kay." Pan flitted over, a golden object the size and shape of an elongated apple in his hand. "Try one, go on."

Kaylen swallowed, his throat dry as Pan gently pressed the fruit into his palm. How did someone who spent their days flying through cold air have such warm hands?

"You've got one for each of us?" El asked.

"'Course," Pan laughed. He pulled a small bag from the boat and handed it over.

They dug in, fingers becoming sticky with the thick pear juice. Pan told them the natural growing conditions, and Kaylen made a mental list of the places he'd be able to sell the seeds.

When he was done, he licked his fingers and looked at Pan. "You had some Lost Ones needin' a lift?"

Pan sighed. "I've been wanting to ask you about that, Kay." He leaned forward, resting his forearms on his legs and pressing his thumb into his palm. As he did so, the golden wings slipped out from under his shirt, the necklace chain glinting at the back of his neck.

A burst of happiness lit up Kaylen's insides at the sight. He shook it off, leaning in as well. "What about it?" he asked with a frown.

Pan hesitated, and when he finally spoke his voice was thick with emotion. "I think I might need you to take all of 'em."

<h1 style="text-align:center">CHAPTER NINE</h1>

<h1 style="text-align:center">Lost Ones</h1>

"All of 'em..." El repeated.

Luke shared her incredulous expression. "That's... aren't some of 'em youngins?"

Pan nodded, not looking at them but at Kay. "They are, I know. It'd be a hard trip to the mainland with little ones, but..." He grimaced. "It's not safe here anymore, Kay."

"Waddya mean?" Kay raised a hand, almost put it on Pan's shoulder, but thought better and rested it on the side of the boat. He looked at Luke and gestured to the goods Pan had brought them. "Let's get this all aboard the ship while we talk. We'll need room if–"

"Aye," Luke cut him off with a curt nod. He clambered back into the other boat, squeezing between bags of seeds, rare herbs and fungi, and the muffins Kay knew Pan would have snuck in for the crew.

"Never Land's never been *safe* for anyone with a drop of human blood, Pan. But you and Tyl said the fairy folk wouldn't hurt the young ones. What's changed?"

Pan released a heavy sigh. Behind him, Zeyda had lifted the oars and was following Luke back to the ship. Both little rowboats bobbed in the gentle waves of the small bay.

"I don't know what it is. But something's wrong. Something in the magic is off. The trees are... they're not growin' the same."

"Looked like they're fallin'" El said, tilting her head and squinting back to the shore. "From the nest comin' in, the eastern side of the island is peppered with missing chunks from the forest. Like bald spots."

Pan pushed his fingers into his hair, resting his head on his hand. "That's something, too. I've heard 'em coming down. The tree fairies wouldn't allow for the way it's happening. The trees aren't sick."

"Is it just the trees, though?" Kaylen's brow furrowed.

Pan shook his head. "That's just the most obvious. The pixies are on edge. Tree-folk, too. There've been queen's guards in the woods. As far south as the Oak. They leave us alone. But for how long?"

He fell silent for a moment. The groan of the oars as Luke and Zeyda moved the rowboats towards the anchored ship were joined by the caws of seagulls and lapping of waves.

Kaylen bit the inside of his cheek. Without Lost Ones on Never Land, Pan would be quite alone. Well, him and the fairy. But he wouldn't need to trade goods with them nearly as often, if at all.

A twinge of that old familiar shame moved in Kaylen's stomach. If the children weren't safe, of course they'd take them. Even if it meant not returning to Never Land.

Pan sighed again, pulling Kaylen from his thoughts.

He sat up, looking Kaylen in the eye. "I know it's not much. Nothing solid. But there's something, Kay. I can feel it."

"You really think the children are in danger?" El asked.

Pan nodded. "I wouldn't ask if I didn't. The Oak will be awfully empty without the Lost Ones."

The sorrow in his voice hit Kaylen in the sternum. He'd never seen Pan carrying this much weight. There'd been bad days, when the flying boy had shared the loneliness of growing–and then not–on an island of fairies. When he'd admitted to Kaylen the remorse he felt for the lives he'd taken when his and Tyl's trips to the mainland leaned into the more dangerous side of adventures.

That had been before Kaylen had met him. Had been one of the reasons Pan had only taken James's hand–not his life.

Even on those bad days, when the two of them stowed away in the captain's quarters to talk, Pan had always carried a youthful air of ease.

As light as the air he was able to fly through.

"We can take them," Kaylen heard himself saying. He almost winced, but kept his face smooth. "We'll find them homes in the islands. That's where we're going next."

Pan nodded, even as El gave Kaylen a significant look.

Helping the ones on the cusp of adulthood find a life among the rest of the world was quite a bit different than finding safe and comfortable homes for the truly little ones.

"Should you come, too?" Zeyda asked, pulling hard on the oars with a soft grunt of effort. "If it's getting dangerous?"

Pan blinked at her.

Kaylen sat as still as glass, feeling nearly as delicate as Pan gave a gentle shake of his head.

"I can't. I can't leave Tyl, and… there's other reasons. But Tyl is the most important."

El shot Kaylen a sidelong glance which he ignored.

"Right," Kaylen said, rubbing his hands together. "Let's get everything on the ship and meet back up. Pan, are the little ones already coming down? Or do you need to fetch them?"

Pan's cheeks flushed. "They'll be coming with the older children."

"Presumptuous," El grumbled. "Ain't even waitin' for the answer."

Kaylen met Pan's gaze and felt the corner of his mouth twitch into a smile.

An hour later the first load of children was headed to the ship. There were only four more, the youngest, who were nervous about the boats and the water and the strangers offering to find them homes.

They were all used to the fairy-folk on the island, so the interesting characteristics of most of Kaylen's crew didn't have an effect. It was leaving Never Land, leaving Pan, that had them hesitant.

Pan helped them into the final boat just as something rocked the anchored rowboat Kaylen and Luke waited in.

The two men exchanged glances.

"Did you–"

"Aye," Luke answered before Kaylen finished the question. He gripped the edge of the boat hard and leaned his head slowly over the side.

The crystal blue water wasn't completely clear, but it was possible to see the fish near the surface, the dark shadows of coral in the deeper parts. And it was clear enough to see the twisting, enormous, lizard-like shape that swam through the water toward the shore.

Toward the children. Toward Pan.

CHAPTER TEN

The Queen

Tyl and Mira found themselves a spot near the dias in the grand hall of the Hollow. The market had closed; stalls boarded up and items tucked away. By the time they arrived at the Hollow, the outside was startlingly empty.

They'd flown over the heads of the tree-folk—standing tallest at the back of the crowd, the pixies—next in line for both height and placement—and now hovered near the stairwell above the heads of many of their kind.

The throne remained empty until it appeared no further fae would be in attendance. As it was, the hall was filled almost to bursting.

A pair of stone doors, which had replaced a curtain of ivy, opened to the side of the dais.

Heads turned. Murmured conversation quieted.

A gnawing sensation rumbled in Tyl's gut. She hadn't eaten yet, but this was something else. A sense. She tried to pinpoint the feeling, digging through her memories for a moment that induced something similar.

Her attention diverted as a handful of fairy guards emerged from the doorway, flanking the queen.

Tyl's gasp echoed through the vast chamber, and Mira pinched her arm to quiet her.

She wasn't alone, however. Many of the fae murmured as the queen flew to her throne.

Queen Titania was a fairy. She wasn't the oldest of the fairies of the Hollow, but she was certainly the most powerful. She'd wielded that power for fairy-kind for centuries.

It had been a long while since Tyl had been back at the Hollow, and longer still–she realized now–since she'd seen the queen.

Titania had grown.

She'd always been larger than the others. Nearly pixie-sized due to the vast amounts of magic she held.

But now... she was tall, taller than a pixie, nearly as tall as a tree-folk. Her features remained recognizable, pale glistening skin, dark hair pinned into curtains along her crown, a dark gown of green flaring at her waist. Her silver wings still fluttered behind her.

But she was no longer the size of the fairies she ruled over.

Part of Tyl took this change with a pinch of hope. Titania had long shown her distaste for the other fae, but perhaps the magic of the island was making her more similar to her other subjects.

That notion was dashed as Mira gave Tyl a slight tug, pulling her back into the shadows of the stair.

Her friend was trembling.

Tyl put her hand over the one Mira had clenching her arm. The presence seemed to settle her nerves.

"Greetings, fae." The queen fluttered up and moved in a slow circle before descending onto her throne. She sat on the edge, crossing one leg over the other and leaning her elbow on her knee as though about to have a relaxed conversation with a friend.

The murmuring in the hall went silent.

Titania gave a nod. "My dears, you must be wondering why I've called you from your various works on Never Land to come to the Hollow. I'm afraid we have important matters to discuss."

Tyl frowned, looking out over the sea of faces and noting fear dotting the crowd.

"Never Land is home to fairies," the queen went on. "Our immortality grants us a natural right to the Hollow and the island itself. And, in our grace, other fae join us, making homes and families here."

She straightened, gesturing out at the crowd.

Toward the middle and back of the hall, the pixies and tree-folk looked rather put-out. The queen's words were not new. She'd said as much when making the decision to block up the Forever Spring.

"But, on occasion," she continued, lowering her hand to the armrest where her fingers curled into a fist, "our guests test our patience and our grace."

Murmurs erupted throughout the hall.

Titania raised a hand and, almost instantly, they quieted. "Take the mermaids, for example. Once living in our cove and enjoying the magic that seeps from Never Land, they pushed the boundaries of our rule and attempted to claim the cove as theirs alone."

Tyl cast a glance at Mira. It was true the mermaids had left years ago, but Tyl didn't recall what the queen spoke of.

Mira shrugged, her eyes wide.

"They're gone now. Expelled for attempting to take more than their share of the magic that flows through the very roots of Never Land."

Mira nudged Tyl, and the little fairy realized her face was scrunched in an incredulous expression. She smoothed her features before someone else noticed, listening intently.

"Unfortunately." Titania shook her head. "Others now aim to don the mantle of *thief* on our island."

A thick weight seemed to settle onto Tyl's chest. She was too absorbed to attempt placing it, but the word came to the front of her mind anyway, unbidden.

Dread.

Whispers picked up again. Fairies glanced around curiously. Behind them, the pixies and tree-folk looked wary.

"Humans," Titania said, her sharp voice ringing through the hall and silencing the fae folk once again.

The dread in Tyl's chest sank like a stone. Her stomach churned at the implication of the single word and, without meaning to, she flew forward a few inches, coming out from under the shadows of the stairs.

The queen carried on, "Humans on our island. You've seen them. Seen the Lost Ones taking from our land. Seen the boy flying in our skies."

Tyl shook her head, anger now rising to join the dread.

"Our magic wanes daily," Titania's voice grew louder. She lifted from the throne, hovering in the air with her hands at her sides, her gaze scanning the crowd. "The trees grow ill and require felling. The springs run dry. The life of Never Land was not meant for the creatures living in the great oak tree."

"That isn't true."

Tyl almost covered her mouth with her delicate hands as the words flew from her lips. She grimaced. But the damage had been done.

Queen Titania turned, slowly. Her assessing gaze took in the now much smaller fairy. She nodded in recognition.

"Tyl, the..." She gave a rueful huff and a cold smile. "The fairy."

The anger in Tyl seemed to burn through the dread. And the caution. She flew closer, her brow furrowed and her hands clenched.

From behind, a calloused hand grabbed her arm, slowing her mid-flight. She glanced back at Mira, her scared face practically begging Tyl to return to their shadows.

"Ahhh, and Mira the spring fairy. How pleasant." Titania smiled at Mira. Then cocked her head at Tyl. "You claim me a liar, Tyl?"

Tyl was a great lover of tricks. If a trickster fairy had been a recognized position by the court, she often imagined she'd have a title after all. But it wasn't, and so she was just Tyl the fairy who was good at tricks.

This trick, however, she did not like. This lie the queen was spinning, of waning magic and human interference. It was dangerous. She didn't understand why the queen was saying such things.

Magic was *not* fading from Never Land. Tyl used it often, and saw it used by many kinds of fae on a daily basis. By the roots, even some of the Lost Ones had shown odd proclivities for bits of magic here and there, likely due to their not-quite-hidden fae ancestry.

Still, as much as Tyl wanted to say yes, the queen was a liar and this was not a very good trick, she was not a fool. If she'd still been like other fairies, with only one emotion working at a time and the current one being anger, she might have flown at the queen for making such a claim. That would have ended with her crumpled body on the stone floor. Or her ashes floating through the air after some burst of magic.

But Tyl was not like the other fairies anymore. With their titles, and their limitations. The anger within her was currently being stifled by worry for Mira and that underlying dread.

Instead of agreeing, Tyl shook her head. "No, my queen. Never. I simply do not understand. The Lost Ones have fae blood in their veins, it's as clear as day when you get close to any of the children. They weren't brought here by ships. They were brought by magic. Surely, that means they belong as much as the rest of us, at least," she glanced at Mira, "at least until they grow into men."

Queen Titania fluttered closer. Behind her, a thin trail of glittering green dripped from her wings. She reached out, putting two gentle fingers to Tyl's small face.

Her hands were cold, the touch like a shock. But Tyl didn't draw back. She bowed her head, as one was expected to do.

"I'm so glad you've asked for clarification, Tyl."

The queen turned away, returning to her dais and her throne. In the intervening seconds, Mira tugged Tyl's arm again, pulling her back, though not quite as far as before.

"We believe there is an answer to this question of where the Lost Ones come from," Titania said. A slow smile twisted at the corners of her lips. "We know they did not begin to arrive until the flying boy, Pan, had lived here for some time."

Tyl's stomach was a tangled mess of knots. She reached out, clutching Mira's hand like a lifeline. No one knew about her taking Pan to the spring. No one. And yet...

"We believe Pan has used dark magic to bring these Lost Ones to Never Land."

Tyl's head felt woozy. The crowded hall erupted into whispers and murmurs. Some curious, some indignant.

"We believe he brought them here," the queen continued, "to steal the magic from our island."

The voices grew louder. Tyl's heart beat against her chest like an angry drum. There were protests in the crowd. Reminders of the various times Pan had used his flight and skill with a blade to save some fae or another.

The queen raised both her hands, but the crowd did not quiet. Her smile turned to a scowl, and she gestured to one of her guards. He slammed the butt of his spear into the stone floor.

The thud was loud enough to break through the noise. When the eyes of the crowd were on her once again, the queen gave a gentle nod.

"I understand your hesitance," she said. "Pan has–"

"Shed blood," Tyl cut in.

Mira's groan behind her was likely audible to even the farthest fae, but Tyl didn't care. She flew up again, not quite to the dais, but higher now so everyone could see her.

She didn't look at the queen. Instead, her gaze met those of the various fae assembled.

"Pan has shed blood for Never Land. He has protected us from creatures of the deep. From pirates who would come and take our people. He treated with the mermaids when they lived in the cove. He's helped tree-folk find and cure root rot. He's aided pixies in their search for rare stones. He's helped to teach fairylings to fly." Her voice rose with each sentence. In volume and desperation.

But they were nodding along. The pixies and tree-folk and even most of the fairies. They knew, as she did, what Pan had done for Never Land.

And it was not what the queen claimed.

Tyl turned, almost expecting to see guards bearing down upon her, but instead the queen was surveying her with a thoughtful expression.

A moment passed. The din in the hall grew, fae calling for Pan to be protected, for the queen to provide proof if she meant to send him away.

Titania raised her hands yet again. "Quiet," she called. "Quiet. Let your queen speak." Her smile, though wide, did not reach her eyes.

The room fell silent.

Titania looked to Tyl and nodded. "Very well. The Lost Ones are to be sent away. Immediately."

Tyl opened her mouth to object, but Titania spoke quickly.

"Pan, however, may stay. The others are a danger to Never Land, but you make a point that Pan has gone out of his way to appear on the side of the fae."

Tyl bristled. She held her tongue, awareness seeping between the pockets of rage in her belly. Guards surrounded the queen. Even more were stationed around the hall.

And, part of her realized that with what Mira had told her earlier that very day, about the spies and the danger, perhaps the children would be safer if they weren't on Never Land.

"The old laws are buried in the land here, as deep as the roots of the Hollow." The queen's voice took on a magical quality, resonating around the grand hall. "Pan may stay. So long as he remains a child, and does not invite another human onto the island."

Tears burned at the corners of Tyl's eyes, and she knew fairy dust must be melting off her wings in waves, so deep and intense was her emotion.

"He won't, Majesty." Mira's delicate voice was just loud enough to reach the queen. "He knows the law. He cares for us all."

The pink fairy gestured to the crowd, and the queen's eyes narrowed again, just a sliver.

After a long moment, she nodded.

Queen Titania turned to the throng of fae. "The Lost Ones have six sunsets to depart. If they are not gone by then, they will face the will of the court."

Tyl stared, but the queen did not look back at her. Instead, with no further refrain, she spun, silver wings taking her back through the thick stone doors to her private chambers.

CHAPTER ELEVEN

Tick Tock

Kaylen had seen the crocodile before, the day his father had lost his hand.

The beast, a massive, primal thing, had swallowed the hand whole. Along with the sorry pirate who'd gotten in Hook's way and been roughly shoved overboard.

Kaylen had had nightmares for a few months after that encounter. Both of the crocodilian creature and his father's rage.

Tyl had talked about fighting the beast since then. It showed up sometimes, often after a bad storm, and roamed the beach as far as it could. The thing was too massive to venture into the woods.

Kaylen's shout ripped from his throat. Pan heard it, turned towards him... saw the beast...

"Row," Kaylen said, his voice cracking over the word. Desperation wetted his palms as he took up one of the oars.

"Kay, we can't go ashore," Luke warned even as his own bark-knotted fingers gripped the wooden oar.

The two rowed hard.

At the beach, the children screamed. Fear gripped Kaylen's heart as the croc finally reared its head out of the water.

Pan was up, in the air and darting to the side. Teeth the size of daggers snapped together where the flying boy had been a second earlier.

Kaylen strained at the oar, urging the little rowboat faster.

The children in the other boat screamed again, sobbing with terror, the sounds traveling across the soft waves lulling on the sand.

Pan fought. With his sword in one hand, dagger in the other, he attempted to keep the croc occupied and away from the little ones.

A slash across the beast's thick back was barely a chip in its armor. Pan flew to the side, narrowly avoiding the spiked algae-green tail as it flew out of the water. The thing was as thick as Pan was, with rock-like lumps forming twin ridges.

Kaylen and Luke were close now. Only a dozen yards from the children and Pan.

Kaylen stood, one hand gripping the side of the boat, the other pulling his sword from the scabbard. He lifted a foot onto the bench and leaned forward, balanced precariously.

"Don't get out of this boat," Luke grunted, his voice strained as he took up Kaylen's oar and continued to push them forward.

The sand was far too near them now. Through the churning of the water and the brief moments of white foam from the waves, the island shore was visible only a few feet down.

Kaylen heard the words, but didn't respond. He knew the rules.

He also knew if the croc got its jaws around Pan, his friend would be dead. Despite whatever fairy magic kept him from aging.

Kaylen watched the beast with careful eyes. When they got close enough he'd be able to draw the thing's attention and Pan could strike it from the back, or fly up from underneath and attack.

The children's boat was on the other side of the beast. Blocked from rescue by the thrashing tail and snapping jaws. All four Lost Ones huddled together between the benches, wide eyes watching, terrified.

"*Oy,*" Kaylen shouted, breathing heavy. He bounced a little on the balls of his feet, adrenaline sharpening his fear into something usable.

The croc, who'd been snapping at the air where Pan darted to and fro, tilted its massive head. Pan flew down its back, swiping with his sword and sending up sparks where his blade met the ridges.

Kaylen shouted again, drawing the croc's attention. The beast moved in, heavy claws stirring the sand beneath the waves as it strode toward them. The push and pull of the little waves in the bay had no effect on it.

Kaylen waited. Like the moment just before the crash of ship against ship, the seconds before impact seemed to stretch and slow. Just as the croc's jaws went to close around the side of their boat, Kaylen swiped.

Blood sprayed across his chest and tunic. His sword caught on the creature and he ripped it free.

A roar of monstrous rage split through the air. The crocodile reared back, bleeding from one mangled yellow eye, the other spun wildly, fixing on Pan again.

The boat lurched. Kaylen didn't dare glance back, but assumed Luke had begun to row them away.

Pan took advantage of the injury, driving forward and slashing at the creature's face and neck.

The croc's tail swished angrily, and to Kaylen's horror, struck the side of the children's boat.

Pan yelled, the children screamed, and one small form tumbled from the boat and into the foaming water.

"Kay–"

He barely heard Luke's protest as he leaped into the waves.

Kaylen's boots landed in the sand, sinking an inch before he charged forward. The water came to his waist, the wicked churning from the croc's massive movements splashing up to his chest on occasion.

The blonde curls of the one who had fallen overboard were slowly sinking even as little arms thrashed against the pull.

Kaylen hurried forward, gripping his sword tight. Above him, Pan dove down, trying for the child.

But the beast was in the way.

Kaylen met Pan's eye. Fear flashed across his face. Kaylen gave a sharp, reassuring nod, moving as quickly as he was able against the force of the water.

He grabbed a flailing arm with his left hand, keeping the point of his blade between him and the croc. He pulled, and the girl came up sputtering. She reached for him with her free hand, and he was able to lift her to his hip.

"It's all right," he murmured. "I've got yeh."

Ahead of them, Pan was distracting the croc. He flew too close to the jaws, and a wash of fear flooded Kaylen's veins. But Pan had been flying longer than Kaylen had been walking, and he avoided the dagger-like teeth by a hair.

Kaylen waded another few feet toward the boat holding the children and deposited the girl inside. The others huddled in the middle still, shaking and crying.

The tow line was coiled at the front. Kaylen snagged it with his now free hand and moved back through the water.

The thick tail came toward him, and he ducked. His hat spun through the air, but the blow missed his body.

The momentum of its tail sent the creature's front half into a spin. Pan cried out as its massive snout clipped his leg. He spun in the air, and slammed into the waves.

With a curse, Kaylen switched hands, hefted the rope, and hurled it with all his strength. The last few feet landed in Luke's lap.

"Get them to the ship," Kaylen called.

Luke said something, probably cursing him, but Kaylen didn't bother to check if his friend was obeying his command.

He turned to face the monster.

CHAPTER TWELVE

Fae and Blame

Pan was in the water. Kaylen pushed forward, the movement an effort against the heavy weight of the sea.

The giant crocodile between them faced Pan. Its long, thick tail swayed across the top of the water.

Kaylen needed to get around it. Get to Pan.

Behind him, the children's rowboat was being pulled—far too slowly but there was nothing to be done about that now—to the safety of the ship.

His pulse thudded in his ears. The adrenaline that came from robbing merchant vessels, fighting slaver ships, and sailing through dangerous waters was a faint echo compared to the way his body was reacting now.

He couldn't see Pan.

Find Pan. That came first. Then get closer to shore. The water was low enough during the dip, but the swell brought it too high for quick movements and effective fighting.

Kaylen lunged into the water, kicking behind him rather than wading through the waves. He swam around the side of the croc. The beast turned, and Kaylen had to dive beneath the surface to avoid a frighteningly large claw.

He came up quickly, blinking and gasping through the drops of saltwater, and searched for Pan.

There.

Pan was conscious, but clearly in pain. He'd returned to the air, one leg dangling at an odd angle, skimming the water.

"Pan," Kaylen huffed, worry thick in his voice.

"I'm fine," Pan said, waving away the concern with his dagger hand. "We have to lure it to the shore. It'll go after the boats."

Kaylen nodded.

Pan flew toward the beach, hitting his dagger and sword together to create a shrill crack. "Hey!" he shouted. "This way, you great ugly thing."

Kaylen stayed on his side of the croc, but did the same, shouting and waving his sword.

On the far side of the croc, the children's boat had finally moved a few yards past the scuffle. Luke strained on the oars. Once they reached the ship, they'd be safe. Even the giant beast was no match for the canons.

But that was a long way.

Kaylen was still moving backwards, stepping carefully with his eyes on the croc. He ducked another snap from the thing's jaws. When it began to pull back, he swiped and cut a line of red into the fleshy bit of scales under its neck.

The water was to his thighs now. His boots sank into the softer sand. He stepped back again and again, until he reached the harder stuff coated with washed up pebbles and rocks. Each step was accompanied by a swipe, duck, lunge, or dart to the side as the crocodile split its attention between him and the flying boy.

"It won't come all the way onto the beach," Pan called. "I can see Luke. I'll tell you when he makes it to the ship."

Kaylen's legs were unsteady on the shoreline. He'd been on the ship a long while, and even the hardest of pirates needed a few minutes to steady themselves when they reached a dock.

"Pan," he shouted back, the strain of the fight in his voice. "Your leg–"

"I'm fine," Pan lied.

And it clearly was a lie, because his leg still hung limp, blood dripping onto the crocodile's back as Pan flitted this way and that to keep it distracted.

Kaylen shook his head, brushed a lock of dark hair away from his forehead, and ducked again as the tail swung his direction.

The beast was tiring. The easy-looking meal had turned violent, and though it likely smelled Pan's blood, it was bleeding as well.

Kaylen took two daring steps forward, and stuck his sword into the joint where the creature's leg met its body.

A roar shook the trees at the edge of the beach. Out of the corner of his eye, Kaylen thought he saw a glint of gold.

He had no time to inspect, however, as the roar was followed by the croc's attention fixing solely upon him.

Kaylen scrambled backward as it took massive steps toward him. He tripped, legs folding across a piece of driftwood as he landed on his butt in the sand.

"Kay–"

Pan's shout was cut off by the slopping sound of the crocodile's massive dripping jaw opening. It bore down on Kaylen, ready to swallow him whole.

Color exploded.

Kaylen winced, covering his eyes with one hand as he continued propelling himself backwards and away from the creature. He kicked the driftwood away, sand coating his wet trousers as he scrambled.

More color. Fireworks of sparks that burst in the crocodile's face. The beast yowled, spinning furiously.

Kaylen flattened into the sand as the tail swiped right where his head had been a second before.

With another angry roar, the croc stomped into the waves, tail swishing furiously to keep the tiny creatures that had attacked it at bay. It waded into the water and dove.

Kaylen rose to his feet, panting, and swallowed hard. Fear thudded with every pump of his heart. He gazed out at the bay, relief finding a momentary home at the distant sight of Luke and the children climbing one of his ship's sturdy rope ladders.

El was just visible in the crow's nest. She stuck up an arm and he waved back. She'd have the spyglass, and so he signaled for them to wait before sending a rowboat back for him.

The crocodile was gone for now, but best not to tempt the thing.

"*Pan!*"

Kaylen's relief vanished. He spun to the left at the recognizable pitch of Tyl's voice. She hovered over Pan, who was on the ground.

Kaylen ran to him, knees thudding into the sand as he reached Pan's side. "What's wrong? Is your leg–"

"I'll be fine," Pan grunted. He lifted himself to a seated position, leaning against a thick cratered rock. "The blasted beast knocked me outta the air."

"What happened?" Tyl demanded. She flitted to Pan's wounded leg, now causing the sand to get clumpy with sticky blood. "What did you do?" Her dark eyes flashed with fury as she glared at Kaylen.

He scowled back at her. "A right lot more than you did. Where *were* you?"

"Busy," came a much softer, yet still pitched voice. Another fairy flew toward them.

Kaylen had never seen this one before. Her bright pink hair reminded him of strawberry jam on a biscuit, complete with little seeds woven throughout.

"It's all right, Tyl," Pan murmured. He smiled at her, a mischievous crease to his grin. "You done being mad at me?"

She scoffed, landing at the hem of his too-short pants and crossing her arms as she stared down at the wound on his leg.

Kaylen grimaced at the damage. Pan's skin was ripped open. A thick bloody gash that would need stitching and a few days without walking.

"I wasn't mad at *you*," Tyl snapped. She rubbed her palms together, glancing at the pink fairy and then back at the wound. "I was mad at the company you keep."

The back of Kaylen's neck itched at her words. Not because they were untrue, but because the familiar bristling of shame was rising up again.

"Tyl," the pink fairy said, flying down to land beside her on Pan's leg. "Be nice." She turned to Kaylen. "I'm Mira. Good to meet you. Pan has told us much."

Kaylen's expression softened into a worried smile. "Can you fix him? Some kind of fairy magic or something?"

Mira gave a small smile. "I can't. I'm a spring fairy. We only make things grow. But this one." She gestured at Tyl. "She'll have her boy up and moving in no time."

"At least up and flying," Tyl added. "Walking will take a few days rest, Pan."

Pan, who'd been growing paler as the conversation went, only grimaced.

Kaylen clenched his fist for an uncertain second, then put his hand on Pan's shoulder. "Good fighting."

Pan chuckled and cocked his head up at Kaylen. "I'd say the same, but I..."

He froze, and Kaylen did as well, hearing the same thing Pan did. An odd tinkling, coming from the trees.

It took the fairies a few seconds longer. Then all four of them faced the forest. Kaylen swallowed.

CHAPTER THIRTEEN

Mortals

"Mira," Tyl whispered, her words barely louder than the lapping waves behind them. "Hide."

Her friend's wide eyes widened further still as she met Tyl's gaze. Mira glanced at the forest again, then a scared shiver made her shoulders dance and she darted away. Tyl's peripheral vision caught where she hid in a clumped pile of driftwood several meters away.

Pan's leg was still hurt. Sticky human blood dripping out onto the sand and staining it a nasty color.

Tyl recalled other bloody moments of their time together: the pirate's stump cradled to his chest as the crocodile munched down his hand, the human girl felled by what Tyl had thought would be a harmless prank, the bright spew of red on the deck of the ships foolish enough to try bringing harm to Never Land.

She and Pan had stopped those ships.

He'd fought, bled, for Never Land. For the Hollow. For her.

"We have but seconds," she breathed.

Tyl jumped from his knee and landed in the wet, mucky sand. She rubbed her hands together and pressed them to Pan's bloody wound.

Tyl the fairy. Just a fairy. But, because she didn't have a place or position, her magic could be used in… special ways. Light poured from her palms.

Pan winced, leg bucking as she snapped at him to hold still.

Strong hands, large as she was tall, gripped him at the knee and ankle. Kaylen only met her eye for a brief second before looking back down at the injury.

Fairy magic wasn't meant for healing. It was meant to make things grow, or to spread frost, or to charge up the wind, or brighten the stars.

Tyl hadn't always been able to heal.

When the girl had laid on the moss with an arrow in her chest, it had been the pixies and tree-folk who had brought her back from the brink of death.

It had been that moment which had solidified Tyl's understanding of the fragility of mortals. That moment which had led her to have Pan drink from the spring. So she might keep him with her always.

And it had sparked her interest in discovering. Another trick. To learn to do magic in ways fairies had never dreamed.

Tyl thought of the girl, of Pan's anger, of her own overflowing jealousy and rage. Of the sadness she'd felt when

Pan had sent her from the Oak. The feelings grew, consumed, and emptied from her fingertips in streams of gold.

The light caressed Pan's wound, blindingly bright for a brief second before it faded into his tan skin.

Tyl swayed on her feet. Her wings fluttered on instinct, keeping her upright. Pan's injury was no small cut. The magic within her felt weakened, drained.

Pan slumped as well. His eyes were closed, mouth pinched in a grimace as he rested his head against the chunk of rock at his back.

"Not bad, fairy," Kaylen murmured. He met her eye, then looked back to the forest.

The tinkling made itself known. A contingent of the queen's guard emerged from the forest, twelve of them, metal platemail clinking together as they flew, the sound growing to an uncomfortable din.

They were different from the ones Tyl had seen at the Hollow. In a similar manner to the queen, these guards were larger. Almost pixie sized, yet flying with fairy wings.

The sight of them sent a shiver up Tyl's spine. Some magic had been used. Either to gift pixies with wings, or to enlarge the fairies. Whichever it was, she was glad she'd told Mira to hide.

Dark metal helms bore down, circling the three of them with an eerie lack of greeting.

"Now what do we do about these guys?" Kaylen asked out of the corner of his mouth.

Tyl stood, wiping her hands on Pan's pants before she took to the air. She spun slowly, marking the eyes, the statures, and the weapons of the guards around them. She recognized none of them; though that could have been because of their coverings and size.

"Greetings," she called, shunting the fear out of her voice and replacing it with a cheery tone. "What can we do for you fine fairies?"

"Careful, Tyl," Pan muttered. He rose as well, limping on the leg but standing tall. The gaping wound was now a jagged scab. It would take another few days to heal completely, if not longer.

She quieted her voice, speaking just to Pan. "Are the Lost Ones..." Tyl pinched her lips together, refusing to allow sadness to interrupt the importance of the moment. "We tried to find them at the Oak. But they were gone. Are they on the ship?"

"Aye," Kaylen answered from behind her. He still knelt on the sand, and she had a feeling it was only because his sword was sheathed that the fairies hadn't been attacked yet. "All of 'em."

She bit her lip. If only she'd been here. She could've dusted the blasted pirate with enough fairy magic to keep his clumsy feet from touching the shore. Of course, if the queen's guards had seen such a thing they'd have arrested her on the spot.

But perhaps they wouldn't have come if he hadn't triggered the spell that covered Never Land.

Her stomach roiled with frustration. It was done. The problem at hand needed to be solved. But, after what the queen had said only a few hours ago, Tyl had doubts that these fairies would listen to her.

She inhaled and forced her lips into a smile. "No need to worry, friends," she called loudly enough for all the guards to hear. "A beast attack, but no harm done."

"No harm?" The question broke the guards' silence. This one was nearly as tall as a pixie. Much larger than Tyl, with soft satiny wings and a shimmer to his helm. "Mankind has not stepped foot on this island without hurting our people in over a hundred years. They are *not* to be trusted."

"I truly mean you all no harm," Kaylen said from the ground. "Coming ashore was an accident. My ship's there." He rose, slowly, and pointed to the bay.

As he stood, six of the twelve guards pointed their spears at him. The others watched with wary gazes, weapons drawn but not lifted.

Tyl grimaced. She faced the guards with their weapons at the ready and put her hands up in a placating gesture. "It's not a problem, really. He was just going. On his way with the Lost Ones, as commanded by her majesty."

The smallest of them—still many times Tyl's size—moved towards her. When he spoke, his voice carried a song-like quality that was out of place with his words. "As commanded? Quick work from Pan, was it? You'd have to have gotten a message to him."

"He's a bright boy." Tyl swallowed. "A bright... child."

Pan shifted, still leaning on his good leg as he watched the events unfold. Tyl had taught him long ago to be silent while she dealt with members of the fairy court. She was glad the lessons had stuck.

"Child." The first spoke again. Brilliant green eyes fixed on Tyl. "A child would fight with such ferocity? A child would, as you claim, protect this island? And was it this," he sneered, "*child* who allowed a full grown human to tread on our shores?"

"I..." Tyl's gaze darted to Pan. Fear took hold, milling about and threatening to overflow. She pursed her lips and forced it down. "He fights for his home, same as we do. And as we've said, the pirate came ashore on *accident*. To stop a beast attack."

The crisp smell of the sea was at odds with the tension in every nook and cranny of Tyl's body. A warm breeze blew over the beach, but she felt cold.

"You know," the large one said, flying forward until he was directly in front of Tyl, "the queen is right. Things on Never Land haven't been the same since that boy arrived."

Tyl's brow furrowed as a flare of anger spiked so sharp and hot it caused a cascade of gold to flow from her wings.

"Tyl..." Pan's voice was soft. A warning? Or a question. It was difficult to discern. Difficult to disconnect the way he said her name now from the way he'd said it as a small boy–scared and lost.

"The pirate is leaving." Tyl squared her shoulders, flexing her wings and rising until her eyeline was just above the much larger fairy's. "The Lost Ones have vacated the Oak." Her jaw worked for a second, but she managed a tight smile. "The queen's will is done."

Behind her, neither Pan nor Kaylen uttered a sound beyond their shallow breaths.

The large fairie, or pixie, or whatever he was, shook his head. "I'm afraid the queen's will extends beyond the removal of the Lost Ones, Tyl."

She floated forward half a step, eyes wide and magic rushing in her ears. "What do you–"

The fairy's gaze slid past her and onto Pan. "Seize him."

CHAPTER FOURTEEN

Broken Promises

Tyl wasn't aware of drawing her sword.

It had been instinct.

Instinct to draw the blade, instinct to raise it to the fairy guard's neck, and instinct to then look over her shoulder to find Pan.

It was the last part which had been a mistake.

The queen's guards launched into action. The one she'd foolishly looked away from struck and, like a tumbling piece of drift wood, Tyl flew to the side, rolling through the air and smashing into the sand.

She screamed upon impact, Pan's name falling from her lips as sheer terror rolled through her.

The fairies were smaller than Pan and Kaylen, but they had magic on their side.

Kaylen lifted his sword as four fairies descended. They hacked. Slicing into him from every angle. He spun, twisting to get them off his back. Each step took him closer to the lapping waves.

Tyl jumped, wings catching her weight as she looked from the pirate to Pan.

Three of the queen's guards attacked her friend. Pan left the ground, injured but still fast. He soared into the air, sword and dagger drawn, but a twisted look of regret aged his face.

"We don't have to do this," he called down as the guards took off after him.

"We do." The fairy who'd struck Tyl met her eye as he advanced.

She raised her sword, snarling.

He didn't bother to lift his spear. Instead, the guard raised a hand and thrust his palm toward Tyl.

A burst of magic slammed into her. She spun again, this time hitting a chunk of volcanic rock. Her left wing gave an audible crunch as it bent on the stone. She cried out, pain sending shoots of light across her eyelids.

"*Tyl!*" Pan's voice carried down to her, and she lifted herself to standing, searching for him in the sky.

On the ground, Kaylen was several feet into the water, swatting with one hand and swiping with his sword in the other. Each time his steel crossed one of the fairies, another would slam him with a similar burst of magic.

A pit of dread grew in Tyl's stomach. This was *not* fairy magic. Not the sparks of light found in the autumn, or shards of ice winter fairies produced. This was something else. Something dark and twisted.

Pan flew high, leading the guards tailing him far above the trees before he flipped and dove.

His size and weight gave the advantage here, and he reached the beach with them a fair bit behind him. He hurried to Tyl's side, raising his sword to catch a blow aimed from one of the few guards still on the sand.

Pan maneuvered with his dagger, disarming the guard of his spear and cutting a line into the armored belly of the fairy. It wasn't a fatal blow, but the guard flew backward as though pulled by a line.

"Tyl," he said again, his voice low this time. "Are you–"

"I'll be fine," she huffed. She lifted her sword from where it had fallen in the sand. With a grunt, she jumped.

And crashed back to the sand with a groan. She knelt on one knee, trying to find the breath that had been stolen by the searing pain in her wing. The pain flashed through her body, deep and profound as more than the wing itself twinged.

"You can't fly," Pan breathed. He met her eye for the briefest of seconds. Tears glistened, magnifying the forest green she loved so much.

"I can still fight," she snarled.

Tyl raised a hand, looking past Pan's worried face and focusing on the guard approaching him.

She pulled from the well of magic within her. A swirl of sand spun like a miniature tornado toward the guard. He fell back, hands raised to block the grains from hitting him in the face.

It was meager, Tyl realized with a pang of hurt. A meager attempt at magic compared to the forces the guards were wielding.

Fairy magic was meant to be specialized, but hers... hers had always been a little bit of everything. Add on how drained she already was from healing Pan–she had no chance of meeting their level of power.

She clenched her hand with a huff. Anger built and crested like a wave within her tiny body. She dropped her sword.

"Enough," a voice cut through the dull thud of her own heartbeat in her ears.

She and Pan looked up as the leader of the queen's guards approached. He flew toward them, a dark glimmer to his gaze. The same one coating his spear, and now his gloved hands. The magic shimmered and shone, moving over him as though it were a snake waiting to strike.

Tyl frowned, a thought hovering at the edge of her awareness, just out of reach.

"You're wanted by the queen," the guard said, leveling his spear at Pan's chest. "You come with us, and the pirate will be allowed to leave."

"*No*," Tyl snapped. She ran across the sand, planting herself in front of Pan.

The fairy cocked his head, expression impossible to read beneath the helm. "Why do you care *so much* about what happens to this human?"

"Why does *she* want him?" Tyl demanded. "We did as she commanded. The Lost Ones are off the island."

The guard shook his head. "It's too late for that now."

"Too late?" Tyl tugged at one of her golden earrings. "That's not..." She grimaced. Swallowed. "Fine. If Pan has to go, so be it." The words burned as they came out. She nearly choked on them, they tore such a gash across her heart. "He can go with the pirates. He can... He can leave Never Land."

In the distance, the sounds of Kaylen fighting echoed up onto the shore. He was being pushed deeper. Magic hit his chest and stomach even as he blocked blow after blow with his weapons. Soon the attacks wouldn't matter. The sea would take him.

The other fairy guards had Tyl and Pan circled again. The leader shifted, as though uncomfortable with what he would say next.

"Her majesty requires an example to be made."

A shiver ran down Tyl's spine.

He continued, "The boy comes with us."

Tyl shook her head, her thoughts on the queen's words earlier that day, of the way the fae had reacted. Of course she needed to make an example of Pan. If he disappeared without warning, he'd be what he'd always been—a mysterious hero. This way… this way the queen would be allowed to write her own story of Pan.

It was an awful trick.

Tyl did not like being tricked.

Pan's voice cut through her rapid thoughts. "What of Tyl?"

Tyl froze, her body cold as though winter had arrived early. Behind her, Pan asked the question again.

"We know the punishment for fighting the queen's guards," he said. "What happens to Tyl if I go with you?"

The magic coating the guard's hands faded to a dull grey color. It reminded Tyl of the queen's wings. He took his gaze from Tyl, looking instead at Pan.

"She is to be banished. The queen knows the extensive list of doings Tyl has done for Never Land. Her benevolence would never allow for such a beloved fae to be harmed…" He paused. "By the crown."

Tyl's breath was shallow. The pain in her wing forgotten as this *impossible* conversation happened. Pan taken. Her banished.

The worst kind of trick.

Pan swallowed, clenching his hands around the hilts of his weapons. "She can go with Ka—with the pirate?"

Tyl's hands shook. She turned around, once again putting her back to the guard, and not caring an ounce as she looked up at Pan. His injured leg trembled.

"You can't, Pan. We don't know what she'll do with you."

Tears slipped down his cheeks. He knelt, one knee going to the ground so he was closer to her. "I don't need to know, Tyl. All I need is knowin' you're safe."

Tyl shook her head. Her insides were no longer swirling with too many emotions to fit. She was numb. Far too aware of her injured wing, her minuscule sword, her empty well of magic, and the size and strength of the creatures who wanted to take Pan from her.

"She won't be harmed unless she continues to act against the queen. Come," the guard commanded. "The fairy may go with the pirate."

"She can't fly," Pan said, his voice soft but firm.

After a pause, the guard looked out to the bay and let out a shrill whistle. Tyl turned to see the ones attacking Kaylen immediately fly up, out of his range, and then back toward the beach.

"Any wrong move," the guard gestured with his spear for Pan to stand. "You'll die first. And then we'll come back for these ones."

Pan rose, taking shaky steps toward the fairy. "I'll fly, if you don't mind."

The guard nodded. "You don't need your weapons to fly."

"Pan," Tyl hissed as he unsheathed his dagger and dropped it and his sword into the sand. "You can't–"

"I think that's enough out of you."

The guard lifted his hand; the grey magic wound itself into a rope-like substance. It flew at her before she knew what was happening. The magic wound around her mouth, gagging her entirely as her fingers scrambled to rip it from her face.

"And for you." Similar chords of dark magic wrapped around Pan's hands, tethering him to the guards on the beach.

They rose a few feet. Pan looked down at Tyl. His face was nearly unrecognizable from the child she'd found on the shore so long ago, so lined was it with sadness and strain.

"A new adventure awaits you, Tyl." A ghost of his usual smile splashed across his face. "Go find it."

He lifted into the air. By the time the magic faded enough to allow Tyl to scream, he was long out of sight.

Chapter Fifteen

The Pirate and the Fairy

Kaylen stumbled toward the shore with weariness dragging at every inch of his body. It felt as though his skin was coated in needles, piercing and poking with every movement.

Deeper wounds, where the magic the fairies had blasted at him had struck directly, were more painful. The lavender amulet around his neck glowed bright with the strain of collecting the majority of the blows.

It would take several days for it to cool down. And, until it did, the magical wounds would ache and burn.

The water pulled at him, and he tripped more than once as the ocean pushed and pulled at his shins.

Why had they stopped attacking?

Kaylen's ears rang. His vision was blurry, and he splashed a handful of water across his face, hoping it would clear the muddled fog in his head.

It did, though with a fresh wave of pain as salt poured into the nicks and slices across his skin.

The shore was red. Blood from the beast still covered much of the sand and rocks, though the tide was coming in, and it would soon be washed away.

As he left the lapping waves, a new sound came into his awareness.

Tyl was screaming. Shrill and high, he hadn't been able to hear it from the water.

Kaylen barely understood. The magic, the pain, the fear of being pulled under by a riptide and drowning while Pan was killed on the shore... his adrenaline had dipped when the fairies left and it took him a few seconds to connect the pieces.

When he did, his legs gave way.

Kaylen crumpled onto the sand beside the wailing fairy. The sound of her cries felt far away. As did the reality that Pan was gone. Surely he'd fly over the trees any moment. He'd race back to them, a mischievous grin on his face from getting away from the fairy guards.

They'd leave together. Tyl too, if she wanted. They'd have a life at sea and maybe... maybe Pan would see Kaylen for more than he was. For more than a slaver pirate's son.

"What..." he finally asked when his voice returned to him.

Tyl was still screeching. The fury encompassing her was not easily released. She darted forward, leaping into the air and slamming into the sand over and over. Her wing, snapped at the top and bent and crumpled at the bottom, refused to work.

Gold flooded from her. Magic pouring from her nose and ears like blood. Some of it was, he realized, as red streaks joined the gold.

"Tyl," he muttered.

She ignored him. Her attempts to fly were beginning to injure other parts. Her knees bled, her tiny hands scraped raw by the sand as she fell again and again.

"*Tyl!*" he shouted. The volume of it seemed to bring her out of her panic.

She rose from where she'd crashed into the sand. Her eyes, dark pools as colorful as the bark of a thick redwood, were streaming golden tears. The ebony flush of her complexion was marred with puffy red bruises from the fight.

Kaylen reached across the sand, his hand closing around the hilt of Pan's discarded sword. "What happened?"

"What..." Tyl spun in a circle, her hands flying through the air with disbelief on her face. "What *happened?* You happened, *pirate.* You're the reason they took him. And now he's..." Her breath hitched on the words. She swallowed and brushed away the tears streaking down her cheeks.

"I..." Kaylen didn't have words for this moment. His heart was cracked. Fractured into pieces at the thought of what the queen might do to Pan. It splintered further at the realization that she was right.

"They'd have come for him anyway."

The voice came from the forest, and Kaylen lifted Pan's sword, shifting himself to block the view of the little fairy in the sand.

The pink fairy - Mira, Tyl had called her - flew out from between the trees. Her pale skin was glistening with the remains of wiped away tears. Her strawberry hair stuck out at all angles and her flowery skirt was torn, as though she'd flown through briars that had caught hold of her.

"What do you mean?" Kaylen asked, lowering the blade and settling back into the sand again.

Mira fluttered close, landing on a stuck up bit of drift wood. She planted her hands on her hips, looking so much like Pan that Kaylen wondered briefly how much of his friend's mannerisms had come from being raised by these little creatures.

Tyl glanced up at Mira, then shot a glare at Kaylen.

He raised an eyebrow. "Want a lift?"

She bared her teeth, but he put his hand down beside her anyway. With a limp that brought a wince to her face, she climbed onto his palm.

Kaylen gently deposited her onto the branch beside her friend.

Mira winced upon a closer look at Tyl. She ran gentle fingers down Tyl's arm, then looked at Kaylen. "I followed them. Tyl, she was going after Pan no matter what. The time she gave you was a cover. A trick to keep the other fae on her side. I doubt she ever planned on letting the Lost Ones leave."

"So Kaylen being here..." Tyl glanced at him, a furrow in her brow. She fiddled with the gold hoops at her ears. "It was luck?"

Mira nodded. "If you hadn't arrived today," she said to Kaylen, "the queen wouldn't have let you come close enough to gather them. It was a trick. An excuse to capture Pan."

"We'd have found a way," Tyl objected.

Kaylen remained quiet, unsure of what they spoke of, but not willing to interrupt to ask.

"I know," Mira said. "But she doesn't. She'd have found something, Tyl. Even without the pirate–"

"Kaylen," Kaylen muttered.

"Right," she gave a dip of her head. "Even without Kaylen setting foot ashore, the queen was coming for Pan."

"Why though?" Kaylen asked. "What does she want with him?"

Mira swallowed, her hands twisting together as she focused in on Tyl's worried face. "To make an example."

A Plan is Made

Kaylen had an inkling that he knew what Mira meant by *example*. But he listened to her explanation anyway.

Mira had followed Pan and the queen's guard. His captors had talked on their way, and she, flitting from tree to tree below and out of sight, had heard it all.

The queen planned to use Pan. To blame the fading fairy magic on his presence in Never Land. She'd kill him to keep power over the various fae. And, because of Kaylen's actions, doing so would be approved–or at least not stopped–by the others.

Pan would die on the spring solstice in four days' time.

Once Mira had heard this, she'd rushed back to the beach.

Kaylen looked out over the water. His ship was there, in the distance as his crew likely debated rowing back to the shore. They'd heed his orders to stay on the ship until he gave the 'all clear.'

Then what? They'd come get him and they'd leave? How could he? How could he possibly leave Never Land after dooming Pan to die?

They sat in silence for several long minutes after Mira finished her story. The urge to venture into the forest stirred like a restless beast in Kaylen's chest. He wanted to cut his way south and find the Hollow. To storm the fairy queen's castle and rescue Pan.

The wounds across his skin, glowing amulet at his neck, and blistered palms from how many magical attacks he'd blocked with his sword reminded him that he wouldn't get far without help.

"How long will it take for your wing to heal?" he asked Tyl, his voice low as thoughts swirled in his mind. A plan was forming. Slowly, with many pieces still missing. But it was something.

She glanced at him. She, too, had been staring out at the sea. He wondered what she saw there. If she knew the dangers one faced on the ocean. Or if she hated it, perhaps because it was where he came from.

Tyl raised and dropped the shoulder on her un-injured side.

Mira walked to her, bare feet dainty on the white driftwood. "Turn," she murmured.

Tyl did as she said, and Kaylen caught sight of the alarm on Mira's face as she took in the damaged wing.

"At least a few days, maybe a week," she said with a heavy sigh.

"Even with it," Kaylen said, his gaze drifting back to his ship, "we'd need more people. My crew are bloody good at sea, and fighters till the end, but there aren't enough of us to take on the queen. Not with those guards."

Tyl looked up at these words. Her dark eyes met his. A steel-like strength resolved in her expression. "We'd need magic. More than I've got by miles and miles."

Mira's eyebrows rose to her hairline as she turned her head from Tyl to Kaylen and back again. "Sorry, you're not suggesting–"

"Magic, huh?" Kaylen frowned, the plan in his mind forming edges, the beginning of a clear picture. "What's the queen got up her sleeve?"

Tyl paced the branch, fingers fiddling with her hoop earrings again. "Fairy magic has been, supposedly, dwindling. But the queen's powers show no such limits, and I'm fairly certain she is able to lend her magic to her guard." Tyl shook her head. "They shouldn't have been able to do what they did here today. I don't know the extent of what she can do, but it's more than me."

"More than both of us," Mira said, her voice trembling.

"No," Tyl snapped, glaring at her. "You're not having anything to do with this, Mira."

"The rot I'm not," Mira snapped back. "I love Pan, too, Tyl. We can't let her..." She shook her head. "I can't even say it." She squared her shoulders and fixed a glare on Tyl. "That boy has been part of our island for more seasons than I can count. He's one of us. Wings or no."

Kaylen cleared his throat. The pale fairy had gone pink, her complexion matching her hair for a few seconds before calming.

"I might..." Kaylen licked his lips, the salt from the sea and the sweat from the fight on his tongue. "I might know a place we can get enough."

"Enough?" Tyl went to cross her arms but stopped with a grimace of pain. She raised one eyebrow as she looked up at him.

He swallowed, memories pounding at him like waves. "Enough magic. Enough to save Pan."

The plan was made and Kaylen's crew called back in the rowboats.

Mira would stay on the island, hiding in plain sight at the Hollow. She'd keep an eye on proceedings and make sure Pan's execution wasn't moved up. If it was... well, she'd think of something.

Kaylen and Tyl needed all the time they could get.

As Mira flitted into the trees, Kaylen turned to Tyl.

"Ready?"

Tyl looked at her hands, still raw and red from her attempts to fly. Then her gaze turned, going to the branches of the tall Oak peeking up from the trees.

"You really think we can find enough magic to take her on? To win?"

Kaylen grimaced. "I don't know about winning, but the place I've got in mind has magic I guarantee you've never seen before, pixie." He let his smile slide back into place at the name.

She glared up at him. "Fine. Show the way then, *pirate.*"

He carried her to the row boat. Luke watched him with wary eyes, no doubt taking in the scorch marks on his captain's shirt, the burning glow of the necklace that protected him, and, of course, the fairy sitting on his palm.

"Captain," Luke said, his expression mild even as his keen gaze took in the extent of the battle without a word. "El said they took Pan. Do we have a plan? A heading?"

"Aye." Kaylen sighed, setting Tyl on the wooden bench in the center of the boat and wrapping a strip of cloth around both of his blistered palms. He picked up the oars and dug into the water. "But you're not going to like it."

CHAPTER SEVENTEEN

Unexpected

The pirate's ship wasn't what Tyl expected.

The last time she'd gone aboard had been in Hook's day. The deck had been sticky with liquor, salt, and blood. The ship as a whole had carried a stench that refused to be washed from one's clothes.

The crew had been different, too. These wide eyes that watched her now were so different from before. These were children, she realized with an unsettled tingle in her spine. Children like Pan was. Young, though she supposed they were old enough by human standards... then again... not all of them were entirely human.

A massive woman with skin paler than Mira and hair white as baby's breath grinned down at her.

"I've never met a fairy before," she said, her voice oddly peaceful compared to her form.

"And I've never met a..." Tyl's lips crooked to the side.

"Zeyda's got orc blood in her," Kaylen murmured.

He stood at the helm, his hands on the wheel and his gaze on the horizon. Tyl was perched on the rail beside him, taking in the changes.

"Ahh," Tyl grinned at the big woman. "Pan and I talked of flying far enough north to see some orcs, but we never did get around to it." She swallowed. "Not yet, anyway."

Zeyda smiled. "It's an honor, fairy."

"Tyl is fine," Tyl said. She inhaled a shallow breath. Pain laced across her wing, down her back, and through her chest. "I'm pleased to meet you."

Four days. Four days to sail wherever it was Kaylen was taking them and get back in time to stop Pan's execution. Ideally, she'd be healed enough by then to fight.

Her hands clenched at her sides. After a few minutes, Zeyda joined the rest of the crew, bustling back and forth across the deck as the ship cut a line through the waters.

"An odd crew," Tyl murmured as she watched a slight woman, darker than she was, scramble up the main mast faster than a human should be able. "Pixie blood in that one?"

Kaylen nodded. "Aye. And Luke is treefolk. And Alexi's got phoenix or fire spirit or something. The rest have less definitive ancestry, but fae kind is what my—" He halted abruptly, hands tightening on the wheel. "Is what Hook was after. Human children got caught in the mix sometimes."

Tyl chewed her tongue for a few seconds. There was something to unpack there. Some story behind his words and the way he refused to say *father* even though they both knew the truth about Hook.

She squinted up at him, her lips pursed. "So you *do* know the difference between a pixie and a fairy."

His laugh seemed to consume the whole ship. It was a barking thing, free and loud, unlike what she'd heard from him before.

"Aye," he said after his laughs turned to chuckles. "I do. But your face takes on such a funny pinch whenever I say it."

She crossed her arms. That *was* a good trick. She stuck out her tongue.

He stuck his out back.

Luke appeared at Kaylen's side a few minutes later. "We're all set, Captain. The children are stowed away below deck, and the crew has been made aware of the change of plans."

"Good." Kaylen stepped to the side, and Luke took the helm. "How many are tryin' to join the fight?"

Tyl cocked her head.

Luke sighed, a wry smile on his face. "It's entertaining as always, Captain, to have to explain to you, yet again, that this crew would go to the ends of the world for you. Fighting a fairy queen to rescue the man you–your friend–is just another adventure."

The word stirred bittersweet emotion in Tyl's chest. Followed sharply by curiosity at Luke's hiccup. As though he'd been about to say something he wasn't allowed.

She caught sight of Kaylen's glare just before the man smoothed his features and turned out to watch the sea.

"I don't know that the crew will be comin' for this one, Luke. I don't like our odds."

Luke shook his head. "We've had worse."

Kaylen glared at him, and Tyl raised an incredulous eyebrow. She doubted very much that they'd had worse odds than fighting the fairy queen in her Hollow.

"Well," Luke amended, "maybe not *worse*. But we're gettin' help."

Kaylen's grip on the rail tightened. "Luke, if they say no…"

"We'll work it out, Kay," Luke said. He grinned down at Tyl. "Besides, I bet they'll be just as curious about our fairy friend as she'll be about them."

Tyl crossed her arms over her chest, frustration chasing everything else from her head. "Care to share *who* exactly I'll be curious about?"

"Not who, little fairy." Luke inhaled, his eyes fluttering closed for a brief second. When he opened them, his gaze was firmly fixed on the horizon. "It's the *what* that'll have you wantin' answers."

⁕ ⁕ ⁕

It took a full day and night to reach the place Kaylen was taking them. He studied the stars as evening fell and, when Tyl asked, he pointed at them in turn, showing her where they were on the map and where they'd need to be to find the mermaids.

Mermaids. Tyl had surprised both Kaylen and Luke when she'd laughed. Of course she'd met mermaids before. Beautiful women, with sharp, almost talon-like hands, black markings on their skin, and long tails that propelled them through the water to hunt.

There had been a time, she'd told Kaylen, when such creatures frequented Never Land. They'd lived near the larger of the two bays, closer to the Hollow. And, when humans attempted to come ashore, their songs had drawn the ships away.

That was long ago. They'd left before Pan drank from the spring, with no warning and no goodbye.

As she dug through her memories, however, she couldn't recall a time they'd used any sort of magic besides their melodic voices. *That* did stir her curiosity.

Her time on the ship gave her an odd opportunity to meet the entirety of Kaylen's crew. It was only ever a handful at a time that ventured in the row boats to meet and trade with Pan.

Each of them carried a fae air to them. It was almost a scent. Something that tingled at the back of her neck and itched her nose. But, as Kaylen had said, most were close enough to human that it was impossible to tell from what lineage they originated.

None of them were planning on missing the coming battle.

"It won't be clever to bring them all," Tyl muttered to Kaylen as the dark blue of the night shifted to dawning grey. "Someone should stay with the ship."

He glanced at her, perched on the rigging beside him. "I know. And I don't want to put any more of them in danger than is necessary." He patted the rail. "We'll need her ready to go as soon as we get Pan, anyway. That'll require hands on deck."

Tyl grimaced. A twinge of sadness battled with anger for a moment until both found a home in her chest.

"I'm sorry," Kaylen said softly.

She frowned over at him.

He shook his head. "Even if we find a way to beat the queen... I know Pan will have to leave Never Land. And for that, I'm sorry."

Her lips crooked up at the corner in a sly smile. "Not too sorry, though."

Kaylen blinked. "Umm."

"I mean," she continued, "it's not as though he'll be alone. This ship is full of adventure. And that's all he's ever wanted."

Kaylen smiled as well, turning from her to lean on the rail and looking out at the slowly rising sun. "We're here."

Tyl raised an eyebrow, turning around as she surveyed the horizon. There was nothing there. No land mass. No sign of anything.

"Are you sure?"

Kaylen chuckled. "I can't forget this place. We're nearly halfway between the islands and the mainland. It's a common enough shipping route, but most captains opt to take a longer trek to avoid certain... treacherous waters."

Tyl balanced on her toes and leapt from the rigging to the railing beside his hand. Her wing twinged with pain as she flung them out to slow her landing. "Why?"

"Why avoid treacherous waters?" he chuckled.

"No." Tyl kicked his hand.

He pulled it back from the rail and pursed his lips at her. "Why can't you forget it?"

Luke sidled up beside them. He was practically Kaylen's shadow on the ship. Always near.

He leaned against the rail as well, meeting Tyl's curious gaze and then staring out at the dark blues and purples replacing the grey on the horizon. "Because this is where we killed his father."

CHAPTER EIGHTEEN

Oddeties

Kaylen grimaced. "You make it sound so dramatic, Luke."

Luke shrugged with a twisted grin. "I'd say pullin' a mutiny and then throwin' two dozen bastards overboard is a bit dramatic, Captain."

Tyl's dark eyes went wide. "This is where…"

"Aye," Kaylen murmured, annoyed that he'd even mentioned the importance of the location. "This is the final resting place of the famous pirate, Captain James Hook."

"Could hardly call him a pirate," Luke growled. "Proper pirates steal from those with too much, not too little."

Kaylen nodded in agreement. On the rail beside his hand, Tyl nodded as well.

A gust of wind ripped up from the sea, shaking the rigging and blowing Kaylen's hair into his face. He pulled it together and knotted it at the back of his head, his mind on that day.

"What happened?" she asked, her voice oddly gentle.

She hadn't been her usual blustery self during the voyage. He'd assumed it had been that nagging worry for Pan in the back of her mind, same as it was for him. His usual jests sat on his tongue, bitter instead of sweet.

He planted his palms on the rail and stretched his shoulders. "Well, the big change was Luke in the hold. He was strong, even then–"

"I'm blushing," Luke interrupted.

Kaylen scoffed and rolled his eyes. "He was strong," he continued. "Strong enough that my foolish fourteen-year-old self figured the two of us could at least take my father down."

Tyl's eyes went wide.

"To kill him, maybe," Kaylen said. "But the goal was to tie him up at least. To convince the crew to release the other children they'd stolen. I couldn't help the ones who came before, but maybe this group…" He cast his eyes at the deck, memories hitting him with waves of guilt and shame.

"None of that was on you," Luke said sternly.

Kaylen shrugged, releasing the rail and sticking his hands into the pockets of his father's coat.

"Kay opened the ale," Luke carried on the tale, speaking directly to Tyl now. "He got the crew drunk, released us all from the hold. It was me, El, Alexi, a few younger ones, and a couple who live in the islands now. We came up with hopes that someone on the crew would listen to reason. But that's not what happened."

Kaylen gritted his teeth. A thunder of sound assaulted his memory. The shouts of pirates–slavers–realizing their catch was free. The fury of his father. The pain as Hook went beyond the normal punishment.

It was as his father had held him against the rail, threatening to send him over the edge of the ship with wild rage in his eyes and hatred spitting from his lips that Kaylen had realized the only way to stop him was to end him.

He'd gripped his father tight, lurched backwards, and plunged them both into the sea.

Tyl gasped as Luke told the story. Her hands flew to her mouth, gaze darting down to the stirring ocean below them.

"How... how did you possibly survive?"

The sun breached the horizon, and a slow grin spread across Kaylen's face as he forced himself back to the present.

"That, fairy, is an excellent question."

The part of his plan that required fairy magic had arrived. If Tyl hadn't come, he'd have had no chance at finding the mermaids again.

They were deep, quiet creatures. Not prone to venturing to the surface often.

He'd gotten lucky ten years ago.

"I can do it," Tyl said with trepidation in her tone. "I just don't know how long it'll last. My magic still isn't as strong as it could be."

Kaylen nodded. "Once we get down there, we should be able to get their help. Ideally you won't need much to get us back to the surface."

"Ideally," the fairy muttered.

Luke crossed his arms, the joints creaking like boughs of a tree during a storm. "I don't like it, Captain. We should send down something else. A cannon ball? A stone? Something that will catch their attention and bring them to us."

Kaylen sighed. He finished attaching a thick length of rope to his belt and grabbed a dagger from the row of them laid out on a crate. He already had one on his belt and one in his boot. "We don't have time for that. Tyl and I will go down. If we're not back by this evening..."

"We sail for Never Land and take down the queen without you," El said with a grin as curved as the blade in her hand.

"No." Kaylen narrowed his gaze on her. "You get the Lost Ones somewhere safe. You keep sailing. You–"

"Enough," Luke interrupted. "We don't talk like that, Kay. You know that."

Tyl glanced at each of them in turn. "You've got to be the oddest pirates I've ever met."

El's dark eyes flashed with mirth. "Then we're doing it right."

Kaylen sighed and pressed his knuckles to his forehead. He looked at Tyl. "Are you ready?"

Tyl echoed his sigh. Her wing was healing slowly. Every few minutes she'd lift herself just enough to hover until a wince brought her back to her feet.

As odd as the crew were as pirates, he'd realized over the last day and a half that she was awfully odd for a fairy. More than once she'd expressed a multitude of emotions at once. She was endlessly curious about the sea and the stars—nothing like the various fairy-types Pan had told him of. And, the oddest of all, she was willing to go this far with humans to help Pan.

She cast a glance over her shoulder and a slight glare at the injured wing. "I'm ready."

He lifted her to his shoulder, and she danced a little on her feet with anticipation.

"Straight down." Kaylen leaned over the side of the ship, staring at the water with nerves like writhing snakes in his stomach. "They'll be there."

She shook her head, earrings swaying, gripping the edge of his collar with her hand and pressing her other palm straight up. "Say it like you mean it, pirate. Maybe then I'll believe you."

He chuckled. She closed her eyes. And Kaylen stepped the two of them off the ship.

CHAPTER NINETEEN

A New World

She'd never done magic like this before, but once she sorted out what was needed, the actual doing was simple enough.

Fairy magic was meant to grow things. Knitting together plant life from its smallest forms. It was meant to change the seasons. Pouring cold into the air or heat into the earth.

Every fairy had a purpose. Every fairy had a season.

Every fairy but Tyl.

She'd thought of how this needed to be done. She'd pull elements from her spring fairy friends, knitting the air into a bubble. From her tree-folk friends, calling on their methods of cleaning the air to keep it breathable. From the winter fairies, keeping a barrier between themselves and the cold they worked with.

It was all similar, yet entirely different.

They landed in the ocean with a plunk. Water splashed up the sides of the almost invisible bubble around them.

The only traces of its presence were the faint lines of gold that flowed from Tyl's hands to the bubble.

"Well," Kaylen said, his voice tight, "that's step one accomplished. Well done."

"Thanks," Tyl said dryly. "I'm *also* glad we didn't immediately drown."

"Next up might be harder." He put his hands out, steadying himself as the orb floated across the top of the water.

"You mean the going down part."

"I mean the going down part." He wobbled.

Tyl inhaled. She closed her eyes again, picturing the magic pooling at the bottom of the orb. She thickened it, increasing the density while maintaining the structure and, slower than she preferred, they descended.

Once it was clear the magic was working and the bubble would continue down, Tyl opened her eyes.

For all her time living on an untamed island surrounded by fae folk, lost children, and sea beasts, she'd never seen anything quite like this before.

When the top of the bubble dipped below the waves, the going became much easier. No longer was her magic fighting against two substances. It was all water now. All the salty sea around them, oddly clear, dark with the sun still so low on the horizon.

They sank. And an entirely new world opened before her.

She was in awe, taking in every new color, every creature that swam past, even a few that had her leaning closer to Kaylen as brief flurries of fear gripped her.

The whole thing was a symphony. A song of movement and color and adventure. A chord that had long been silent, so long she'd forgotten to listen for it, struck in her heart.

"This is... almost unbelievable."

Kaylen nodded, his hands still held up, fingers almost touching the orb for balance. "This is what I saw the day I died. Made it almost..." He swallowed. "Almost not so terrifying."

"You died?" Tyl demanded, turning to look at him for a second before facing ahead again, focusing on the magic and the sea.

"Aye. We both did."

She swallowed, knowing who he meant and feeling a rush of guilt in her stomach at the way she'd treated him. At the words she's spoken in Pan's ear about a man she clearly hadn't known at all.

"The mermaids saved you?"

He nodded. "They brought life back into me. And then their counterparts ridded us of the rest of Hook's crew."

Tyl frowned. "What do you–"

But her words were cut off. Drowned out by a sound that sent shards of ice into her very essence.

A song.

Haunting and beautiful. Golden and cursed.

Figures emerged from the darkness around them. An array of faces, some beautiful like the mermaids she'd known in Never Land. Some with eyes too wide, teeth too sharp, and features odder even than the fae of her island.

Tyl swallowed, her hand tightening again on Kaylen's collar. "Please tell me this is who we're looking for."

He inhaled, blowing out a breath and straightening. "It is," he murmured. Then, louder, "Greetings. We intrude upon your peace seeking help."

One of the dozen creatures surrounding them swam forward. Her tail was long, longer than legs would be if she were a woman. It glistened in the low light filtering down from the surface, a silver thing with streaks of green almost like veins glittering across her scales. Her eyes were the same green, too far apart on her face. She turned her head, fixing one eye on Kaylen.

"You intrude, that is true." The creature–for Tyl was not entirely sure which of the beings before them were mermaids and which were something else–sounded as though she was speaking down a long tunnel. The bubble they were in distorted her voice. "We've helped you once, pirate. What makes you think we'd help again?"

Kaylen swallowed and licked his lips.

Tyl's spine tingled with nerves. Her wings shifted reflexively.

"When you saved me as a youth, it was because you believed my story about wanting to stop a danger to these waters. My story hasn't changed. My crew works to keep whaling ships, slaving ships, and fae hunters away from your people."

Tyl jerked around to look at him. Fae hunters... she hadn't heard of such things in a long time.

A different creature, one of the more human-looking ones with flowing golden hair and a tail the color of spider's silk swished closer, tilting her head at them. "You keep dangerous men from these waters?"

"Aye." Kaylen's face paled.

Tyl's brow furrowed.

"You keep our meals away, then," she said.

The one next to her, with odd features and pointed teeth, rolled her eyes. "Your kind get plenty to eat closer to the mainland, Kendara. That is not a grievance to put upon the boy."

"He's a man," Kendara snapped. "I'll put any grievance I choose upon him."

The other turned so quickly that Tyl flinched.

Her tail swished and she shifted forward, her face inches from Kendara's. "Then explain why he cannot hear your song. Hmm?" She looked back at their bubble. "He is pure of heart. Which means you can float *quiet* during this conversation, or you can take yours elsewhere to hunt."

Kaylen's breath was shallow, and Tyl felt him trembling under her bare feet. A brief thought of what it must have been like ten years ago, when he'd gone into the sea, gone under, and had to face these beings alone...

She shook her head. "I beg an allowance for my naivety," she said, looking at the one with the green tail. "I'm familiar with your friends' kind. We used to have dealings with mermaids at Never Land–"

Around them, each creature with those odd eyes snarled. Their teeth bared, hands clenched around weapons or into fists. Kendara and the other, more human-looking ones chuckled. She brushed her hair back with a hand and exposed a thick black mark across her chest.

"My sisters often lie," she said with a grin that didn't make it to her eyes. "These ones," she offered a limp gesture, "are the mermaids. My kind... the *pretty* kind–"

This brought a new round of snarls from the others.

She smirked and continued, "are sirens. Pleased to meet you, fairy. I believe I know some of the ones who used to frequent the Never Land bay." Her smile shrank into a scowl. "Until that queen of yours banished them."

"That's why we're here, actually," Tyl said, her voice low but not as trembly as she felt. "We need help stopping her from killing someone very important."

"A fairy?" the *actual* mermaid asked.

"A human," Kaylen answered. "An immortal one, or as close as humans can get to it. He's important."

"To whom?" Kendara scoffed. "Another mortal? Or a fae?"

His breath caught, only for a moment. Tyl met Kaylen's eye then. A quick look that confirmed every suspicion that had been growing on the ship. There was longing there. Longing and despair and heartbreak.

And she was angry. Angry with her little fairy body and her compressed fairy emotions and her lack of awareness because there was always *something else*. Always a distraction.

She'd seen that look in Pan's eyes only a few days ago. And she'd completely dismissed it.

"To us both," she returned, her voice stronger now. She turned from Kendara, meeting the mermaid's eye instead. "We've come for magic to save him. And more, for magic enough to stop the queen."

CHAPTER TWENTY

A Lesson in Magic

The sirens left. They scoffed at the thought of helping a human, and more specifically a man. With vague threats of when they'd see him next and to be careful for *someday* he'd hear their song, they were gone.

Tyl was glad of it. She hadn't interacted much with the ones at Never Land. The ones who'd lied about being mermaids. She wondered if they'd been different from Kendara and her ilk. But then again, they'd been responsible for many shipwrecks before they'd been banished.

The mermaid introduced herself as Asira. She asked a few simple questions about the magic Tyl had used to create the bubble, then offered to provide them with something more comfortable.

Kaylen flashed Tyl an alarmed look, but there was something about these creatures... something in the way their eyes watched Tyl and Kaylen, not as something to guard against, but something to protect... made her unnaturally trusting.

"Hold your breath, mortal. Just for a moment," Asira said.

Kaylen inhaled, his shoulders rising, and Tyl grabbed his collar hard.

"What about–" she started to say. But before she finished the question, the mermaid pressed a hand against Tyl's magic. The bubble broke.

Water slammed in, and Tyl cringed, curling herself into Kaylen's neck. Instead of being crushed by the weight of it, the water surrounded them like a blanket. It swirled, closing in and then spreading to give them a breathable area larger than her bubble had allowed.

The sand, only a few feet below them, opened up and Kaylen dropped onto it. He landed on his feet, one hand going to his shoulder to steady Tyl.

"That was something," he murmured. "You all right?"

She shrugged. "They certainly have more magic than I do." The thought did not bring her any happiness. Instead, the familiar feeling of jealousy crept in.

Around them, the mermaids floated upright, just outside the barrier that kept the water away from her and Kaylen.

"Aye," he muttered in agreement.

She glared at him.

"Please," Asira said. She gestured a hand, fingers webbed to the first knuckle joint, at a clump of volcanic rock on the ocean floor. "Take a seat. We have much to discuss."

⁓⁓⁓ ⁓⁓⁓

The open ocean surrounding them felt wrong. Not because Tyl didn't like it–if anything she felt more free here than she had in ages. No, it was because their mission almost seemed as though it needed more covertness. As though part of her thought the queen's guard might have followed them out to sea. As though they could be watching at that very moment.

A foolish thought for a myriad of reasons.

Tyl gave herself a little shake. Her wings extended on instinct and the pain of her left one sharpened her focus even more. Her thoughts abandoned Never Land and what might be happening there as she returned to the moment at hand.

"What do you know about fairy magic?" Asira asked. She was just before them, perched on the same chunk of rock but on the water side of the barrier she'd formed.

Tyl frowned. "I'm a fairy. I know a lot."

Asira nodded with a chuckle that made Tyl squint at her. "Understood. What do you know about *other* magic types, then?"

Tyl licked her lips but hesitated.

Kaylen answered instead. "The fae all work in different ways. There's inherent magic. The ones who have it in their bones and blood." He pressed his hands together. "It draws on them."

Asira nodded.

Kaylen carried on. "Then there's the kind that pulls from the ground. Takes power from all the *things*. Trees, rocks, the soil itself. Even the sea."

The mermaid grinned, her sharp teeth sending a shiver down Tyl's spine.

"Then there are ones who can imbue. I don't know where they get their magic, but they can put it into other things." His hand went to the amulet around his neck. Its glow had faded over the last day and night, but it hadn't died entirely.

Tyl tapped his jaw and he put his hand up, giving her a way off his shoulder. She leapt from his palm when it was close enough to the rock, landing with a partially covered wince at the way the cold, salty air stung her injured wing.

"Fairies can do that," she said, looking from Kaylen to Asira. "We use the magic in us to imbue the growing things we care for. Most fairy magic is dedicated to caring for the land."

Asira nodded. "Most."

The back of Tyl's neck tingled. How much did this creature already know about her?

"Well done, pirate," the mermaid continued. "You're better educated than most on the subject."

He waved away the compliment. "My crew knows more than me, but they've taught me a fair bit."

"That does cover most of the kinds of magic," Asira said. "Not just for fae, though ones of fae bloodlines often find that magic comes easier to them. Some others can learn it." She cast a glance at the other mermaids now patrolling the exterior of the little air cave Tyl and Kaylen sat in. "Though that is also disputed. Perhaps the mortals who use magic have fae ancestry we simply don't know about."

"I have the kind of magic that comes from me," Tyl said. "It drains when I use too much, and it takes time to fill again. All fairies run on this kind."

Asira shook her head. Her green eyes glinted with knowledge Tyl was now itching to understand.

How did larger creatures handle this? This encompassing array of emotions that hit all at once and warred for space?

Or, Tyl bit her lip, maybe their emotions didn't war. Maybe they had room for more.

The thought had her feeling a bit left out, which crowded against the desire to understand, which made her angry on top of the rest.

She scowled. "The magic that *takes* is forbidden among our kind."

Asira inclined her head. "That's true. But it doesn't stop certain fae from using it, does it? There are orc settlements to the north that target villages because they've sucked magic from the very rocks under their feet and have nothing left. There are pixie clans on the volcanic isles that have torn away the heat from the ground to gain power and now the warmth of their islands is gone."

Her eyes narrowed. She leaned forward, planting a hand on the rock and moving so close her head moved through the barrier. Her voice, though clearer now without having to pass through water, was raspy and rough, as though the air grated on her throat.

"Your fairy queen is headed the same way, little one. She started with outsiders. That's why the sirens left. But it didn't take long for her to turn to the island itself."

There was a long pause as Tyl held her breath, unable to process the words. The mermaid stared at her, those green eyes glinting not with malice, but a question.

"The barren gaps," Kaylen murmured.

Asira sat up, returning to the water while Tyl reeled, her heartbeat thudding impossibly fast.

"What?" She turned to look at him.

"When we sailed in," he said, louder this time. "El saw it better than we did, but there are chunks of Never Land missing forest. Not the coves or the valley, either. But places that were definitely dark and green before. Whole sections are gone."

Tyl swallowed. Her thoughts rushed so quickly it was like the sound of the roaring ocean in her mind. The valley that had once been dotted with trees. The fear Mira had of being overheard, seen by prying eyes. The stone consuming the Hollow.

The queen and her guards, larger than any fairy before.

And the magic... the magic fading from Never Land.

She doubled over, breaths coming quick and shallow as her realization turned to fear, to fury, and began to overwhelm her tiny form once again.

Chapter Twenty-One

Bargains

Tyl's sudden panic attack–and he recognized immediately that's what was happening–had Kaylen entirely unsure of what to do.

If it were El, or one of the others on the ship who occasionally faced the monster of their minds when it turned on them, he'd take their hand. He'd press it to the mast. He'd tell them to curl their toes into the wood of the deck. To smell the sea air. To taste the salt on their lips.

But this was Tyl. The little fairy who sometimes thought he was funny and sometimes hated him. Maybe hating more often than the other.

Still, he had to do something as her tiny form doubled over, breaths erratic and wings fluttering with gold spinning off them despite the one still wounded.

"Hey," Kaylen's voice was low but firm. He reached out, putting his hand before her. "Squeeze my hand. Breathe."

She glanced at him, all the animosity disappeared from her gaze. She reached out, taking hold of his pinky and squeezing.

"We don't have time for this, little one," Asira said. She'd returned to her side of the wall keeping the ocean from destroying them. Her voice, once again, sounded far off and deep. "Your queen has more magic than she has any right to. More than she should be able to hold in her form."

Tyl spluttered a moment. Her wings fluttered, and she lifted an inch from the rock before settling back down. "She's changed," she choked out. She sucked in a breath, the pain on her face melting into anger. "She's grown."

Asira nodded as Kaylen's eyes widened. "That makes sense. It's been going a long while now. She's taken much from that island."

"So, what do we do?" Kaylen asked, desperation leaking into his voice. "Pan, she took him. He's got his own kind of magic... or something. But will she..." He swallowed.

It was Tyl who settled him. She put her hand on his once again, pressing into his palm. "She's trying to make an example of him. That's what Mira said. To use him as an excuse for why Never Land is losing magic. She wants to kill him."

Asira sighed. "This will be the flying boy?"

Kaylen nodded.

The mermaid shook her head and directed her attention at the fairy. "If you truly want the power to save your friend... it will come at a great cost."

A memory stirred in Kaylen's mind. A rumor on the wind. Muttered words that circled in communities that boasted witches.

"Whatever the cost, I'll pay it," Tyl said. Her panic was gone. Replaced again with the fury he recognized.

A soft, bittersweet smile crossed Asira's lips. "Even if it means you give up being a fairy?"

⚬⚬⚬⚬⚬⚬ ⚬⚬⚬⚬⚬⚬

Tyl's blank expression offered no insight into what she might be feeling, but the gold pouring from her wings suggested it was more than her body could contain.

"Bargains." Asira rose from the rock, swishing back with her tail and swimming in a short circle before returning. "Bargains are more powerful than any form of magic we've discussed so far."

Kaylen pursed his lips, thoughts going to the cargo on the ship, the coins hidden at various ports, anything he might be able to trade.

"Not that sort of bargain, Kaylen." Asira's voice was gentle. "This is not magic you can buy for gold or gems. This must be an equal exchange." She cast her gaze down on Tyl. "It may be more than you are willing to give."

There was a long pause during which Kaylen contemplated just how much of his mind the mermaid was able to read.

She caught his eye and gave a sly smile.

He swallowed and looked back at the tiny fairy.

Tyl had been watching the mermaid, but now looked down at her hands. She drew the needle of a sword from her waist and stared at the thin blade.

"I found Pan on the shore when he was as little as the smallest of the Lost Ones. He might have swatted at me. Might have chased me into the forest. But he didn't. He watched me. Stared for a long time before he stood up on those fat little legs and followed me away from the water."

She licked her lips.

"We've battled sea monsters, traveled to distant lands, stolen and tricked and fought pirates." Her gaze darted to Kaylen and back to her sword. "Every adventure, by each other's side. Even when we..." Her words grew almost too quiet to hear. "Even when *I* made mistakes."

Her brow furrowed as she looked back at Asira. "What do I have to do?"

Asira nodded. "To start, you let me teach you a fair bit more about the kind of magic you'll be using. Then you make a decision."

Tyl nodded.

"Bargains are *the* most powerful kind of magic. Because there is no limit, see? A person with everything might trade wealth for power, but the wealth doesn't matter. A person with nothing still has their life, their blood, their bones, their memories, their heart and soul... You don't draw strength from yourself with a bargain. You draw strength from the magic of the bargain."

Tyl stepped closer to Asira. "The more powerful the item traded–"

"Powerful may not be the right word," Asira corrected her gently. "The more valuable the thing traded, the stronger the magic will be. To fight Queen Titania..."

"My wings," Tyl murmured.

Asira nodded.

"I give you my wings, and the bargain will give me the magic I need to stop the queen."

CHAPTER TWENTY-TWO

Wingless

Tyl's wings buzzed with what felt like electricity. The salty air stung at her skin. No. It wasn't the air. Wasn't the sea spray she loved so much that was causing the tight, ripping sensation across her arms and legs and torso.

It was mourning.

She gasped lightly at the realization. Mourning for the wings she hadn't yet parted with.

She'd said the words. Promised her wings to the mermaid behind her. And now came the time to follow through.

"This will hurt," Asira said.

Tyl looked up, meeting Kaylen's wide amber eyes. He masked the alarm quickly, but she caught it. Caught the reflection of a blade made of bone behind her in his gaze.

She'd offered to take them off herself. To cut a piece of her off without help because maybe that would add to the magic.

Asira had explained, gently, that the one who made the bargain was the one who had to collect the wings. "You give me your wings, I give you magic. The bargain ties us together. I must be the one to remove them."

"For Pan," Tyl whispered, her plump lips pursed as fear made her heartbeat flicker faster than a hummingbird's.

Kaylen nodded. He reached out his hand once more, and she placed her palm against his.

"Deep breath, little one," Asira said. "I'll be quick."

And she was.

The speed with which the mermaid sawed off Tyl's wings was a mercy. The pain that came with the act was beyond anything she'd imagined. Beyond anything she'd ever be able to explain.

It broke her, cracking her skin and fracturing her mind and splitting her into two.

One Tyl, who had been a fairy.

And one who no longer was.

She collapsed to her knees, the scream erupting from her breaking through the barrier of water and sending a rush of sea towards her and Kaylen. She screamed again, reached out a hand on instinct, and the water halted as though frozen in time.

The pain grew.

It shouldn't have. It couldn't have.

But it did.

Her whole body tore. Skin ripped as she fell from the rock and landed in the wet sand. Hands caught her fall, stopped her from hitting the ground too hard.

She flinched for a moment, certain that in her state of pain she'd missed the moment fairies had found them.

For it had to be fairies gripping her shoulders tight. It had to be hands the size of a strawberry bud lifting her to sitting.

They couldn't be the hands of the pirate who had brought her below the sea to save the boy they both loved.

"I did not think it would happen so fast," Asira was saying to Kaylen. She shook her head, tail swishing furiously on the other side of the barrier. The mermaid no longer had control over it.

The barrier belonged to Tyl now. It had broken with the force of magic released during the cutting of her wings. And she had reformed it with pure will.

She looked down at her hands, her pale palms and dark skin. The places where her nailbeds had cracked. The skin on her hands was healing. Dark splits fusing together and leaving her smooth complexion in their wake.

Red sleeves drew her eyes to the jacket she wore. She stared down at it. The gold buttons glinted as the water above them shifted and refracted the light. Kaylen had wrapped it around her, she recalled. Had gently helped her arms into the sleeves and left her to do the buttons as he'd looked away.

"I knew you'd grow," Asira admitted, looking across to where Tyl stood. "I thought it would take months. Years even. For a normal fairy, it could have taken decades. It wouldn't have hurt. Not that part, at least." She glanced down at the small glittering gold wings clutched in her hands.

They were, Tyl realized, absurdly small. How had those held her up? How had they allowed her to soar through the air as though riding the wind?

"Why did it happen all at once to Tyl then?" Kaylen demanded. He stood close to her.

She'd fallen twice so far. Legs unsteady. She hated that they were unsteady. She walked plenty as a fairy.

But there was weight missing. As light as her wings had been...

She shook her head, focusing back on Asira's words.

"... different about her," the mermaid was saying. "Fairies can only carry so much in their bodies. It's possible–"

"It's all been straining the edges for some time now," Tyl murmured.

The pirate and the mermaid both turned to her.

She met their gazes, then looked up at the surface where a ship waited for them. "The... everything, really. Has been pushing at my insides for a while."

Asira gave her a thoughtful nod but said nothing.

"Are you all right, though?" Kaylen asked. He reached out a hand, met her eye, and looped his thumb into his belt instead. "Do you have the magic? Are you able to fight the queen and win?"

Tyl looked to the mermaid. The two shared an unspoken expression. A knowledge that settled in Tyl's stomach and almost seemed to balance her weight.

"I have the magic," she said to Kaylen. "We should go back."

CHAPTER TWENTY-THREE

Drawing Straws

The change in Tyl was stark, fierce, and unsettling.

He couldn't think of an alternative to what they'd done. But part of him wished they'd not gone to the creatures of the deep. He worried she'd traded more than just her wings for the magic she now held.

They were back on the ship and headed to Never Land. If the wind held true and the tides were kind, they'd arrive the evening before the execution.

Tyl stood at the prow of the ship, staring out at the water as the sun set off the rear starboard bow. She watched the water with an intensity he knew but did not understand.

When the work of the captain was done, the ship settled and steady, he went to her side.

"Now I really can't call you a pixie," he said, putting a touch of his usual teasing tone into the words.

She didn't look at him. The ends of her curly hair shifted in the wind, a scarf keeping the rest pinned in place. Her clothes, borrowed from one of the crew, fit her well.

Even without his jacket–which he'd gotten back as soon as new clothes were made available–she made a half-way decent pirate.

"I suppose not." Her voice was deeper. Less of a birdsong now. "It's all different."

He nodded and leaned against the rail. "I didn't know, Tyl. I hope you believe that. I didn't know this," he gestured at her tall form with a limp hand, "would be the price."

"I'd have done it all the same," she said, turning to lean her hip against the rail and facing him. "And I'm still calling *you* a pirate."

The familiar wicked grin that split her lips brought a rush of relief to his chest. She was still there, after all. The fairy, hidden in the...

"What are you now?" he asked.

She raised an eyebrow, and he winced.

"Not... you know what I mean. You're not Tyl the fairy. You're not a mermaid. And, as much as mankind would be honored to have you..." he sighed, thinking about the black lines he'd spotted on her hands when the change had first occurred. "I don't think you're quite that either."

The smile returned. Not wicked but certainly thoughtful. She looked down at her hands. A scattering of golden sparks ran across her palms before she clenched them into fists. "No, I don't think so. I'm not sure. We can decide what to call me after we get Pan away."

"Away? Is that the plan then?"

She sighed. "I think it has to be. I have powerful magic, yes, but we don't know how deep Titania's magic goes. I doubt I'd be able to kill her."

He tilted his head. "There's always a chance. We'll probably catch her off guard when we arrive. I doubt she'll be expecting you to show up twice her height and with more magic than a regular fairy can dream of."

"Ha," Tyl chuckled. "True. And yet, I fear a fight the magnitude required to end her would put all of Never Land in danger."

"You're worried about casualties."

She nodded, though it wasn't a question. "The fae didn't ask for her to turn tyrant."

"So our aim is to escape?"

Tyl stretched her neck. She'd been doing that since they'd surfaced. Her hand reached up and rubbed at her shoulder blade.

Kaylen's stomach twinged.

"Our aim is to get Pan out. That'll be your task. Mine will be to distract her, or kill her. Or..." she drifted off for a moment, her brow furrowed. "Perhaps there's a way to quiet her power for a while. She wasn't always like this, you know."

He was quiet for a moment, thoughts turning to his father. Hook *had* always been a mean bastard, but his malice hadn't been directed toward Kaylen until he'd been old enough to question Hook's cruelty.

The sound of the ship cutting through the water below them filled the silence.

"I've flown over the sea." Tyl's voice was so quiet he almost didn't hear her. "Pan and I have a few times. But this has a different feel to it."

"The ship?"

She nodded. "The ship, the crew, the feel of the waves through the deck."

Kaylen smiled. He leaned into the wooden rail of the ship, picking at his nails as he looked out at the rolling waves. "We go to port often enough, but land has never really felt like home. Even with all the old memories here..." He cast a glance at the door to his quarters.

"I didn't realize you'd been the one to kill him." Tyl twisted the golden ring on her pinky. It had been one of her hoop earrings before she'd grown. The other one was gone, lost to the sand.

"I didn't mean to be," Kaylen murmured. "And at the same time, I wish I'd done it sooner."

She turned to him with a fading grin. "Pan told me you were a child when we met. Were you still one when you took the ship?"

He blinked at her. "I... yes. It works differently at sea, plenty of boys crew ships, but by mainland standards I was a child."

"The queen isn't my mother," Tyl said.

Kaylen opened his mouth, then closed it again.

"I don't have one," Tyl continued. "But I think for any fairy, she'd be the closest we've got. She was different when I was little."

He huffed a chuckle. "Mine was a bastard from the start. But it still felt like I'd betrayed some part of myself."

"Well, I've already done that." Tyl gestured to her wingless back. "What comes next is about Pan."

He didn't say anything. Didn't think she needed him to. Instead they stood together in silence, watching the horizon as Never Land grew closer.

⁂

The pink fairy met them at the ship with confirmation that they hadn't come too late.

Though they'd known the execution wasn't set until the next day, the fear that they'd arrive moments after the worst had sat deep in Kaylen's chest the entire way back.

Darkness covered the bay. The moon's light was dim, just a sliver of white reflecting off the ocean. Dawn would arrive in a few hours. And with it, a fight like nothing Kaylen had experienced before.

He pressed his fingers to the amulet around his neck. It was cool once again, the heat of the magic it had absorbed dissipated.

"The queen will do it in the Hollow," Mira was saying. Her small form paced on Tyl's open palm as the crew gathered around to listen. "She wants a spectacle. And she's expecting Tyl to intervene." She looked up at her friend. "She knows you'll try something, but there's no way she's planned for... well..."

Tyl let out a wry chuckle. "I'll be a surprise as I always am. There is no planning for Tyl."

Kaylen let out a laugh. It took Mira a second for the worry to flip to mirth, but then she chuckled as well.

She explained the ins and outs of the Hollow with occasional help from Tyl, as well as the timeline for the execution and following festivities. Then the fairy and former fairy settled onto the stairs and continued talking in low voices.

"You're not going alone." Luke's deep voice cut through Kaylen's internal planning.

The captain turned to look at his first mate. "I'm aware. Tyl and Mira are going as well."

"That ain't what I meant and you know it. You're taking some of the crew."

Kay raised an eyebrow. "Aren't I the one supposed to be giving orders?"

"Only while they're making sense."

Kaylen glared. That wasn't entirely true, and Luke knew it. There'd been more than one adventure that had required trust in plans Kaylen either couldn't, or wouldn't share with the crew.

Kaylen did, begrudgingly, understand that this wasn't one of those times.

He moved away from the others, one hand on Luke's arm to bring his friend along. "I won't put the lot of you in danger for my own selfish pursuits."

"Ye've got too much book-learning to call yourself selfish for this one, Kay. We all like Pan well enough, and we're not blind nor stupid." He tilted his head, the bark-like texture of his skin casting odd shadows in the candlelight. "You care for him. Why would you not want yer crew comin' to help you rescue your true love? Like in the storybooks?"

The heat that flushed Kaylen's cheeks and neck almost made him worry his amulet was malfunctioning. He ran a hand through his untamed hair, nearly pulling out a few strands in frustration.

"It's not... I can't, Luke. I can't put you lot in that position. And I can't... he's not like me, see? Not a pirate. Not the son of a..."

Luke gripped his arm just above the elbow. "I know you're not speaking ill of my captain, Kay. You're more than a pirate. More than the son of that piece of shite. And more than good enough for the *flying boy*." He said the last words with a grin and an emphasis, as though remembering the stories passed along the crew in the gap of years before Kaylen had gathered the courage to return to Never Land again.

"It's going to be dangerous," Kaylen said, shifting his body as quickly as he attempted to shift the conversation.

"Aye, we've never dealt with danger before." Luke gave him a lazy grin.

"Not the normal kind," Kay snapped. "This'll be magic. Fae folk with power beyond ours."

Luke's grin slid into a scowl. "Fae folk who left their kin to the mercy of men like yer father just because we've got human blood as well. There are a few of us, Captain, who have our hurts to heal through steel."

Kay hefted a sigh, his insides churning with worry and guilt. "I won't... I can't order any of you to come with me."

"Yeh don't have to."

"And," he put up a hand, "I can't let you all come. We need people manning the ship and the row boats."

Luke shook his head, his hand moving up to rest on Kaylen's shoulder. "You underestimate my organizational skills, Captain."

He gestured to the crew, and Kaylen realized that a number of them were gearing up as though preparing to take a ship. Others were prepping the row boats, and others still were checking the rigging to ensure the ship was ready for a quick departure.

Luke leaned in, his mouth crooked up in a grin. "We've already drawn straws."

CHAPTER TWENTY-FOUR

What Are You?

The sun rose too quickly. Not abnormally so, but Tyl had been hoping for a misty morning. For a fog that might disguise their arrival and slow the process of the fairy court in preparing for Pan's death.

The rowboat had landed on the sand when the sky was still grey. Kaylen's boots hit the ground with an ominous thud. The second rowboat waited near the ship, bobbing in the water unnoticed.

Mira sped away before the queen's guard arrived. Only four of them this time, likely because the rest were preparing for the festival. And execution. The conversation was brief. None of them seemed to recognize Tyl, but they'd been expecting an intrusion of some kind and were prepared to bring the pirates before the court for sentencing beside Pan.

Kaylen and Luke were disarmed. Tyl spread her arms and moved in a slow circle, still slightly unbalanced, to show that she carried no weapon.

The sky to the west was a crisp blue, to the east dark red brightened to pink as Tyl, Kaylen, and Luke were marched to the Hollow.

The market was abandoned. Quiet, but for the quick footsteps of those stragglers hurrying to join the throng inside.

The queen's guard did not have to speak to move the onlookers. The crowd parted for them at the entrance, fae moving away from pirates being led to the dais.

The Hollow was full. Crowded with every sort of fae to be found on Never Land. Pixies clustered near the entrance, beady black eyes wary as they surveyed not only the pirates, but the fairies as well. Treefolk found their places in the areas closest to the wooden trunk. A few of them were surveying the sap which bled from the various places marble and stone had replaced wood. One touched a bit of the sticky substance, tears welling in her eyes.

The fairies, whom she'd expected to look the most comfortable, seemed unable to hold still. A soft fluttering of wings brought a twinge of pain to Tyl's back. As though her flesh was angry still about what had been given away.

Tyl walked behind Kaylen and Luke, the scarf covering her hair doing a good job of hiding her face as well. Still, her presence did not go unnoticed by every fae folk they passed.

Her old teacher, Finch, caught her eye from the edge of the crowd and stared for a long moment with the expression of someone trying to place a face. When they'd passed and she'd lost sight of him, she caught the sound of his gasp.

To her surprise, a slow smile crept across her face. This was, after all, a trick. Maybe her best one yet. The smile grew.

Trickles of gold fell from the wings of a few fairies she recognized. The ones like Mira, who spent their time away from court, living in the forest and caring for the plants and creatures of Never Land.

They were anxious.

This was not the way fairy festivals usually went.

Tyl pulled the scarf lower around her face. Avoiding recognition until the final moment would be helpful. Not only for saving Pan, but also for the tickle in her stomach at how well her trick worked.

Mira flitted forward as Tyl and the pirates reached the dais. She landed on Luke's shoulder, her trembling fingers gripping the sharp fragment of bark that stuck out from his ear and almost gave him a fairy-like appearance. He and Kaylen seemed calm, but their hands twitched at their sides. Neither had been keen on giving up their weapons.

Tyl put a hand to her hip where, a day and a lifetime ago, a sword had hung.

Chatter fell away as they reached the dais. The guards who had marched them in moved back, forming a semi-circle behind them.

In front of them was the dais, more guards, and the queen.

And not just the queen. Kaylen's low growl echoed the buzz of anger skimming along Tyl's skin.

No wonder the fairies moved like agitated bees.

Queen Titania sat on her throne, her back straight as a sapling, pointed chin raised, crown on her brow as heavy-looking as ever. She held a scepter in one hand, the stone at the end sharpened to a serrated point. Her other hand rested, almost lazily, on the arm of her throne. Long nails, painted to look like the marble she was so fond of, tapped against the stone.

The sight of *her* hadn't caused Kaylen's anger, or the buzzing of the fairies, or the fury compounding in Tyl's chest.

No, it was the crumpled form at her feet that produced the ire hanging in the air.

Pan sat on the cold floor of the dais, hunched with his back to the throne and his head bowed. His wounds from the fight on the beach had healed, as Tyl knew they would. But new wounds, fresh bruises, cuts across his arms and chest, had Tyl clenching her hands into fists. He was chained, a manacle around his ankle keeping him grounded.

Forget magic. She wanted to strangle the queen with her bare hands.

Her vision blurred for a moment, the heat of anger threatening to overwhelm her. She inhaled, nostrils flaring. But the breath did what it needed to. She remained calm. On the outside, at least.

"Interesting." The fairy queen uncrossed her legs. As she sat forward, her gossamer silver wings unfurled behind her.

She looked at Kaylen, her gaze not yet finding Tyl.

Her tone was lackadaisical, as though she hadn't a care in the world. "My guards let you live, pirate. You dare set foot upon Never Land after such mercy? And with more mortals."

Kaylen didn't speak.

Tyl glanced his way, unsurprised to see him trembling with barely controlled rage. His hand clenched at his waist, where his hilt should be.

The queen didn't seem to notice. She shook her head, a smile curling at her lips. "You've doomed yourselves to die with him." She gestured to Pan.

He looked up at her words, his eyes glossy and lost.

A crack threatened to split Tyl's heart. The pain of seeing her friend there did not drive away the anger. It mixed with it. Fused with it.

Tyl moved to step forward between the men.

"Aye," Luke murmured, his low voice a warning. A reminder to stick with the first plan as long as possible.

Tyl knew better, though. The plan had been folly from the start.

There was no peaceful resolution. There was no grabbing Pan and getting out without swords drawn.

No. This was going to end with bloodshed. So why not start things off by wiping the queen's cursed smile from her lips.

"You'd execute this boy?" The sound of Mira's voice cut off Tyl's movement.

The small fairy left Luke's shoulder, flitting forward hovering before the guards blocking their way.

Murmurs went up in the crowd.

The queen's eyes narrowed. She cocked her head at Mira. "What of him? Does a spring fairy care more for an intruder who steals from her people than she does *this court*? Do you side, perhaps, with the *traitor?*"

Mira swallowed. Her pink skin paled, but she straightened, hands clenched at her sides as she turned to the crowd. "I am a spring fairy. One of the Hollow folk. One who was raised under leaf and bough. Which means I know Pan."

Tyl's mouth was dry, her hands clammy with sweat at how close Mira was to the queen's guards. This was the first plan. The one that wouldn't work. And yet, Mira's ability to combine conviction with a gentle tone had Tyl hoping it might.

"I've known this boy from the day Tyl brought him up from the shore. He may not be a fairy, but he is as much a fae folk of Never Land as the rest of us."

Gasps peppered the Hollow. Muttering grew. Some of agreement, some scoffs of discontent.

"Hear me," Mira called, her small voice amplified by the height of the hall. "You know him, too. You know him not as one who steals from us, but one who protects." She spun slowly in the air, looking out at the crowd. "Who kept us safe when slavers came to our island? Who drives away beasts from the northern shores? Who cares for the Lost Ones? Who aids the pixies and treefolk to the north–" she cast an angry look at the queen, "as *we* once did?"

"So you admit he's a thief then?" The queen's voice was calm, but Tyl did not miss the twist in her lips before she spoke. Nor the way she was watching Mira fly. As though she were a cat about to pounce.

Tyl opened her hand, the magic in her heeding the call in a fraction of a second as it pooled in her palm.

"I–"

"He stole the duty of the fairies, did he not? To watch over the other fae?"

Mira shook her head. "The fairy magic–"

"*Also stolen.*" The queen stood from the throne, and continued upwards. She rose higher than Mira, staring down at the little pink fairy. "*He* is the reason the magic of Never Land fades. *He* is the reason our lands turn against us. With his death, our home will return to its full glory."

"*Lies,*" Tyl hissed. She stepped forward, pushing between Kaylen and Luke to glare up at the queen. Her hands were folded before her, magic crackling across her palms.

In the silence of the Hollow, her voice echoed.

Titania paused. She cocked her head and turned slowly to look at Tyl. "And what would a..." She hesitated, unease flickering across her expression. "Ohh, interesting again. A day of new developments."

She swept her hands wide, laughter coming forced and stiff from her lips. "Some of you might recognize Tyl the fairy. Or... at least she used to be. Tell us, did Pan cause this? Did he steal your wings?" She shook her head, disgust in the twist of her expression.

"No." Tyl said. "Pan has stolen *nothing*. From me or any other fairy–"

"You aren't." Titania waved a hand, as though flicking Tyl away. "You aren't a fairy. You don't belong in the Hollow any longer. Not now that you're a..." She frowned. "What *are* you?"

A shiver ran down Tyl's spine. She'd wondered at that. And she wasn't sure she had an answer. Not yet.

She stepped forward, her lips drawn up in a scowl that showed her intent. "It doesn't matter what I am. You're *not* going to hurt my friend."

And she blasted the magic in her hands directly at the queen's face.

CHAPTER TWENTY-FIVE

The Battle Begins

T he attempt for diplomacy ended as quickly as he'd expected. Tyl's ability to hold her emotion in check had been a nice surprise. It, plus Mira's interjection, had given his crew time to get into place.

As Tyl moved forward, exchanging words with the terrifying creature who'd hurt Pan, the rest of the plan—well, the secondary plan—clicked into place.

Tyl's declaration, accompanied by the explosion of magic, kicked off the fight they'd all known was coming.

The queen flew back as a burst of magic slammed into her face. Screams erupted from the crowd. Guards jumped into action.

And above them, El emerged from one of the many open arches in the tree. A handful of crew did the same, scurrying out and down, slashing into steel-covered guards on the way.

More crew poured from the various entrances of the Hollow. Pirates, swords and daggers at the ready, circled the dais and kept the guards busy.

"Captain!" El called, catching his eye and grinning.

He exhaled a breath, allowing worry to eat his insides for the briefest of seconds before El cackled and tossed his weapons.

His sword, and Luke's, clattered to the cold stone floor. Kaylen scooped them both, handing one to Luke and giving El a sharp nod.

El spun away. Her dagger work was quick, thin double-sided blades spinning through the air and into guards with enough force to knock them backwards.

Kaylen shoved past the confused guards before him and leapt to the dais.

Luke followed, scooping Mira from the air and tucking her against his neck with a gruff instruction to hold on.

As Kaylen knelt beside Pan, Luke took up a ready stance at his back.

"Pan." Kaylen's voice came in a ragged whisper. He'd felt panicked enough when the guards had closed in around them on the shore, but that fear was nothing to what had hit him when Pan had stared up at them with blank eyes.

"You dropped this, my friend," Kaylen said with a desperate attempt at humor to bring Pan out of his haze. He pulled Pan's dagger from his boot, the one discarded in the sand when the fairy guards had taken him, and pressed it into Pan's hand.

The blade clattered to the ground, and Pan's gaze slid past him, unseeing.

Kaylen exhaled, worry tight in his chest. "We're here. You're safe."

He set his cutlass on the stone, fingers grappling with the thick chain cuffed around Pan's leg. Dark runes glowed red, and his skin blistered where he touched the metal. "By the deep," he cursed. "It's enchanted."

"Let me," Mira called. She practically fell, her flight was so quick. She darted to the cuff, rubbed her hands together, pulled something from the little bag at her side, and shoved it into the hole of the lock.

"It's magicked," Kaylen repeated. He gripped his sword with one hand, the other gently touching Pan's cheek.

He was cold. Cold and dazed and injured.

No matter. Kaylen shook his head, plotting the return trip to the bay in his head. He'd carry Pan if need be.

"Dark magic," Mira said shortly. She planted her hands on the metal. Acrid smoke rose, her flesh burning as she grimaced and refused to pull away. "Has nothing on the power of growing things."

With a blinding flash of green light, the lock erupted with greenery. The seed she'd shoved into the keyhole exploded into life, branches of a sapling ripping through the metal lock. The cuff fell open.

Kaylen gripped Pan under the arm and pulled him away as the tree's roots twisted into the stone of the dais with shattering fury.

The two collapsed to the ground. Kaylen covered Pan as stone chipped and flew.

Luke yelled, a shout that pulled fear anew into Kaylen's heart. With a worried look at Pan, still dazed and unseeing, Kaylen leapt to his feet.

Across the dais, Tyl and the queen fought with the sort of magic he'd hoped never to witness. Stray blasts from the queen struck straggling fae attempting to flee the hall. Some of the creatures collapsed into ash. Others roared, growing twice their size and taking on distorted, twisted features.

The ones who changed didn't seem to care who they attacked.

Blood pooled at the entrance to the Hollow.

Tyl held her own with the magic she'd bargained for. Gold spun and wove, like roots in the earth her glittering power pierced the air and snaked toward the queen.

More than once, Kaylen was sure she'd land a critical blow, but the queen would launch, not at Tyl, but at one of his own crew.

The lot of them had descended. They battled the queen's guard and the magically twisted creatures. Swords smashed against each other, daggers flew through the air, they missed more often than not with how quickly the winged fairies moved.

Each time it looked as though Tyl was about to strike a blow to bring the queen out of the air, she was forced to alter course, throwing shields of glittering gold in front of Kay's crew.

The pirates were well equipped and trained. They battled the guards back, enchanted gems and weapons collecting the worst of the magic those smaller fairies sent their way.

He was torn, frozen in time for the briefest of seconds as he took in the battle. Help Tyl or join the fight against the guards?

Logic smacked him upside the head with the realization that any attempt he made on the queen would only force Tyl to protect him as well.

The guards. They had to remove the guards from the equation.

His crew were scattered. Injuries grew as dark magic flew through the air and steel cut through defenses.

Kaylen ran. Not with the speed of a boy brought up by a caring family, by a loving mother who rocked him gently, or a father who kept him fed and clothed.

No, Kaylen moved with the deftness of someone brought up on a slaver pirate ship by a bastard who quite enjoyed the pain in others.

El faced off against two of the larger fairy guards. Kaylen's blade danced in the air, slitting through the wings of one with no twinge of regret. He gripped the other's arm, heaved, and flung the fairy in the stone ground.

A sickening crunch sounded. The scent of blood, thick moss, and various types of smoke–scorched flesh, burned clothes, and something acrid and noxious—coated Kaylen's nostrils.

El flashed him a dark grin, then scampered off to help another crew member.

With a thick barrier of ice firmly fixed around his heart, Kaylen shifted his sword tip into the space between the fairy's armor, and drove his blade into his chest.

Kaylen spun, locking his gaze on a new target, and rushed to attack.

The fray turned in their favor. The crew shifted like a wave, blocking the queen's allies from her side and cutting them down one by one.

Kaylen's stomach lurched at the number of bodies on the floor. Some were crew, scorch marks burned across their skin where the queen's guards' magic had found openings.

The Hollow was nearly empty now. The remaining fae watched with bated breath. And Kaylen hated them for it.

They watched. Not to help. Not to stop the queen from destroying everything Never Land meant. But to decide where they stood when the fighting was done.

A low growl escaped his throat.

Behind him, back near the dais, Luke shouted.

CHAPTER TWENTY-SIX

Boring Days

Tyl and Pan had a game they played when things around Never Land got boring. He'd fly, as fast and agile as he was able. And she'd fire harmless bursts of gold seed magic at him.

The seeds would explode on contact, showering the boy in glittering dust.

It had been a favorite for both of them, but they'd fallen out of the game as their adventures grew. As they faced more and more danger, and the boring days became a different kind of exciting.

Tyl twisted her arms, raising the right beside her face as the left extended toward the queen.

The magic in her now, bubbling like molten ore, roaring like an angry sea, was not harmless. She hardly needed to call upon it for it to flood her veins. Her hands glowed, fingertips sparking with power.

She and Queen Titania spun. The queen took advantage of the air and darted this way and that to try and knock Tyl off center.

But Tyl hadn't adopted a human boy and taught him to fly without learning exactly how to read another person's movements. Jagged shoots of root-like gold spun through the air. They grazed and scratched and burned the queen.

But it wasn't enough.

For every strike Tyl managed, the queen sent off a scour of shots toward the pirate crew who'd risked their lives to save Pan.

And *rot* on him. Rot on that boy who'd taught her to care about more than just the two of them. Who'd taught her to feel pain when the Lost Ones cried. Who'd taught her to feel joy when they helped someone in need.

She threw up shield after shield. Bark-like chunks of light that rebounded the queen's magic.

A few still got through. And Tyl's magic... deep as the well within her was... started to fade.

She leapt to the side as another burst of gray sludge from the queen's pointed scepter smashed into her own throne and carved a chunk from it.

Titania cackled, her voice hoarse and strained. "You can't keep dodging, you little disaster."

Tyl grunted, shoving up from the ground and throwing a bolt of her own magic at the flying queen. It hit her ankle, the smell of scorched flesh adding to the thick mossy scent of fae blood that had filled the Hollow.

"Me, a disaster?" Tyl snarked. "What do you call a fairy queen who steals magic from the fae?"

The queen hissed.

Tyl fired another blast, aiming high to drive the queen down.

It worked; Titania dove too vigorously, crunching into the ground with a yelp.

Tyl threw another molten chunk of magic at her.

Titania conjured a grey shield as Tyl hit her with another and another. Hand over hand, arms aching from the force driving through her bones. She gave no breath, no room to stand or flinch or prepare.

"Dead," Tyl spat, her own breaths shallow and forced as she did not relent the onslaught.

The queen's arm was above her head, the smoky shield she'd created fading quickly.

Victory burned hot in Tyl's belly. It roiled up her chest as she lifted her hands for one final blow that would, at least, destroy the queen's defenses. Dry up the poisoned well of magic inside her.

"The fae belong to *me*." Titania screamed it with magic behind her voice. Deafeningly loud, her words echoed through the Hollow, shaking the very tree itself.

Tyl winced. Something warm and wet trickled from her ringing ears.

But her magic was ready. She need only break the defenses. She need only get close enough to touch the queen—with Titania's magic drained, she might have success in knocking her unconscious. And if not... Well, that was what swords were for.

Tyl slammed her magic into the queen's shield. It exploded in a burst of ash.

The force of it blew Tyl back; her head cracked into the side of the dais. She groaned. Lifted herself onto one arm.

Her vision danced for a few precious seconds. Was that a sapling above her?

A calloused hand reached out. Her sight sharpened as she took it, the familiar feel of bark under her fingers, and Luke pulled her to her feet.

She met his eye with a grim, determined pinch on her brow. He nodded, understanding.

It wasn't done. Not yet.

The queen had flown back as well, crumpling against the stone stairs pressed into the wood of the Hollow. She stared at Tyl, rage blazing in the dark depths of her sunken eyes.

"The fae are mine, you foolish thing." Queen Titania let out a vicious laugh. "When you had him drink, you made him mine as well." Her voice carried through the hall, magically distorted, and sent a shiver of dread through Tyl's veins.

Something shifted not far from her. She turned.

Pan rose from the ground. His chains were broken. His eyes were no longer cloudy and vacant. They'd taken on the same muddy black hue as the queen's.

In his hand was the long dagger Tyl had stolen for him years and years ago. He looked at her, no recognition in his gaze.

He lunged.

CHAPTER TWENTY-SEVEN

Hazel Eyes

Luke's shout pulled Kaylen's gaze.

Horror split him in half as Luke leapt forward, putting himself between Tyl and... and Pan.

The flying boy sliced, cutting across Luke's shoulder and sending a spray of all too mortal blood splashing across the ground.

Luke cried out, stumbling sideways.

Kaylen spun, panting as he yanked his sword from the body of a guard who'd attempted to split his throat open with magic. The amulet at his chest burned white-hot. It seared his skin through his shirt, but he didn't dare remove it.

He scrambled up the crumbling side of the dais toward Pan and Tyl and Luke. Splintered light from above cast the broken stone with odd shadows, and he stumbled in his hurry.

Why? Why would...

The question burned away at the sight of Pan's eyes. They were unseeing. Dark and vicious as though he struck with intent, but his expression was blank.

"Tyl?" Kaylen shouted the question as Pan went to strike again.

In a fluid movement, Kaylen slid his sword between the dagger and Luke's side.

His tree-like friend staggered to the side, grunting. Kaylen glanced back, only for the slightest second as Pan pulled the dagger back and struck again.

"I've got Luke," Mira called.

Kaylen barely nodded as Pan's dagger came toward his head. He dodged to the side, sliding his sword up and causing Pan to parry. Whatever dark magic had taken him hadn't gotten rid of his skill with a blade.

The edge of Kaylen's sword slammed into the dagger's cross-guard, just stopping the blade from slicing into Pan's arm.

Kaylen's breath came ragged through parted lips.

"Keep him distracted," Tyl shouted.

He shoved, pushing Pan backward. He flew through the air, spinning before righting himself the way Kaylen had seen him do so many times before. But there was no mischievous smile on his face now. No mirthful laugh.

Only blank expression and deadly intent.

"Tyl," Kaylen called back, his voice wavering with anxiety. "I can't fight him without hurtin' him."

Her voice sounded just behind his ear, as though she was inches away instead of sprinting across the hall towards the queen. "Her defenses are gone. I have a plan. I need only touch her, and it will be done. Hold him off until then."

Kaylen nodded. He inhaled, furrowed his brow, and strode toward Pan.

The flying boy had paused, hesitating in the air to watch Tyl run towards the queen.

"Hey," Kay called, throwing a taunt into his tone that made his stomach squirm. "Down here, Pan. Let's see who the better swordsman is, aye?"

It was unfair, Kaylen knew, as Pan darted toward him with the dagger flashing. He had a full sword, and Pan only had a long dagger. The odds of such a fight were remarkably in his favor.

Or they would have been if Pan couldn't also fly and Kaylen weren't trying desperately not to hurt him.

The first lunge on Pan's part was a feint. Kaylen darted back, but a kick caught him in the temple.

He staggered back, dazed.

Instinct put his blade ahead of him just in time to block the flash of steel as Pan flew at him. He shoved hard, sending Pan backwards.

Kaylen spun, pulled his own shorter dagger from his boot, and faced Pan again. He inhaled through his nose, attempting to steady his shallow breaths as worry and adrenaline pumped through him.

Pan's brown curls were damp with sweat. The bruising across his face was accentuated by the shafts of light pouring in from the open branches of the Hollow.

He flew at Kaylen.

In a swift movement, Kay twisted his sword and locked Pan's blade in place between his own dagger and longer sword.

The point of his dagger scraped Pan's chest. Kaylen grimaced, but easing up would mean Pan's blade piercing his collar.

Pan squirmed, bringing his fist down on Kaylen's head to try and loosen the blades. Kaylen lost an inch and cried out as steel pressed into his flesh, drawing blood that soaked into his shirt.

He pushed back, the blade easing out of the gap just below his collar bone. He grunted with effort. Jaw tight. Breathing shallow through clenched teeth.

Behind Pan, Luke and El approached slow and silent. When they reached him, they'd be able to subdue him. Hold him down until Tyl ended the queen, or finished the spell, or did whatever she'd need to do to free Pan of this.

There was a crack. Loud enough to ring Kaylen's ears. A burst of air, or energy, or magic hit them both with the force of a wave. Knocked them sideways.

The pressure was gone faster than should be possible.

Pan's dagger clattered to the ground. And Kaylen's...

Kaylen's dagger protruded from Pan's sternum as the flying boy's eyes returned to the warm hazel Kaylen had fallen in love with.

Chapter Twenty-Eight

Blood for Blood

Pan had attacked her. Or, tried to, before Luke got in the way and took the strike meant to end her.

He was fighting Kaylen. Fighting Kay as she struggled to get her feet steady under her. Her head spun from the way it had cracked against the stone.

But Pan needed her. Needed her to end this and break whatever cursed spell the queen had put on him.

She ran.

Kaylen's call, that he couldn't fight Pan, couldn't hurt him, found her ears. She whispered a response, shooting it toward him with a pinch of magic to keep their plans a secret.

The queen was weakened. Her magic was drained. She was standing, panting, against the side of the hollow.

Cornering her did not make her any less a threat.

Titania grunted as Tyl approached. Her glistening wings fluttered. Her feet left the ground.

Tyl slammed into her with the full force of her human stature.

They both went down, sprawled across the stone floor. Tyl scurried towards her, magic heavy in her wrists, ready to be used.

Titania flipped around and struck. The jagged point of her scepter jammed into Tyl's side.

Tyl screamed as pain erupted through her, the sharp stone driving through her skin. Blood flung across the stone floor. The queen scrambled to her feet and lifted the scepter again, her arm shaking with the effort.

Tyl's scream morphed. Shifted. Became a cry of determination and rage as Tyl took hold of the scepter and ripped it from the queen's hand.

Titania stepped back, panting. "You can't kill me," she spat. Her eyes were wide, glistening with crazed rage. "You're not strong enough. You could slice me to pieces, and I will still come back."

"I know," Tyl breathed. "Every waking breath from you would mean my destruction." She moved toward the queen.

The queen gave a snarling smile. "Yes." She shifted her wings, attempting to unfold them after being crunched against the ground.

"It would mean..." Tyl spoke between heaving, exhausted breaths. The fingers of her left hand tightened around the scepter. "The destruction of my kind. The end of the fae."

The queen's smile faltered. Her gaze darted to the weapon and then back to Tyl. "Leave here," she snapped. "Leave Never Land and live. I won't hunt you."

"No." Tyl swallowed, her feet carrying her the final few steps until she stood before the queen. "You won't."

Her dark hand, the color of earth perfect for planting, for growing, for life, closed around the queen's neck.

❧ ☙

A wave of magic roared through the Hollow. The sound was too loud. The force too strong. And yet, Tyl held Queen Titania firmly in place.

The stone the queen loved so much began to take root. Tyl's magic drained, pouring through her hands as it coated Titania, binding her forever to the wall of the Hollow. Encasing her in stone. Turning her from flesh, to a sleeping statue.

Tyl's arms shook. The scepter fell from her limp fingers. There was no room for second guessing or doubt; this magic would work. It had to.

The stone crept away from Queen Titania, crawling across the walls and floor, curling up the inside of the tree and fusing with the inner trunk in an unnatural, magical fusion.

The Hollow would do some of the work in keeping the queen contained. She would sleep, frozen in stone, for a thousand years.

When it was done, Tyl found herself on her knees before the statue.

Wincing, she pushed herself up. "I don't like not having wings," she muttered, pain cutting through the words.

She looked at the queen again, wariness in her guarded gaze.

But the fairy was still. Still and unmoving. Frozen in time.

Tyl turned away from the queen, the flush of victory rich in her cheeks, even with how exhausted she was. She pressed a hand to the wound at her side.

Pain radiated through her body. It felt as though she'd been left out in the sun, dried like a piece of fruit, shriveled and empty.

The magic would return. Not as strong and plentiful as it had been from the bargain she'd struck with the mermaids. But it would return. Someday.

Until then, her injuries would have to heal the slow way.

Tyl pressed the slice carefully, glad to see the blood flow had already stemmed, as she headed toward her friends.

Her footsteps slowed as she approached. She faltered, eyes widening at the sight of Kaylen holding...

"Pan?"

Kaylen looked up at her, tears streaming from his eyes, mixing with the blood and ash on his face as they fell through his scruff and dripped from his jaw. "He... he went limp. He didn't... I didn't..."

Pan groaned, pain dancing across his face. He shook his head. "Wasn't your fault."

The dagger in Pan's sternum was Kaylen's. Tyl recognized it. She tilted her head, disbelief blocking sound and emotion from reaching her.

She knelt. Her hand went to Pan's cheek. He'd drunk from the fountain. He couldn't die...

But that wasn't true. Fairies before him had died. The fountain protected him from aging like a mortal. It didn't stop him from being wounded beyond repair.

"Pan, I'm so–" Kaylen broke off, his grimace cut with grief and shame.

"Not you," Pan murmured. "I know you."

Tyl's knees were wet. She looked down, taking in the blood seeping through her clothes as though it were an odd piece of art.

This wasn't real.

"We won," she stammered. "We beat the queen. This isn't..."

Pan leaned his head into her palm. "I'm proud of you, Tyl. Little Tyl." He chuckled, the sound hoarse and rough as blood dribbled from his lips.

She shook her head again. "Mira, the pixies, the tree-folk." Tyl looked around.

The pink fairy sat on Luke's shoulders, hands covering her face as she shed silent tears.

Tyl's heart wrenched a little further at the sight of her friend's bent wings. She knew that pain well.

"They're gone." Mira's breath hitched in a sob. "I'm sorry, Tyl. I don't have... I can't."

Tyl scanned the Hollow. Mira was right. Bodies littered the stone; guards, monsters, and a few fae. The rest had fled.

Kaylen looked at Tyl. "Do you have anything left? Any magic at all?"

Tyl swallowed.

She looked down at her hand, the black cracks along her nailbeds had grown, crawling along her fingers past the first knuckle joint. That emptiness inside her ached. Not a drained cup anymore. This ache was worse. It was a glaring reminder that there was nothing she could do to help her friend.

Pan let out a shaky sigh.

Kaylen ran his bloody fingers through Pan's curls, desperation painted on his face as he read Tyl's answer in her expression.

Then his brow furrowed. He looked down at Pan, the dagger slowly draining the life out of him. The blood pooling on the stone under them.

"The most powerful kind of magic comes from a bargain," he breathed.

Tyl's eyes narrowed. "Yes."

Kay reached for Pan's dagger. It lay in the blood, the handle dripping as he lifted it. "A bargain needs a trade."

Luke took a step forward. "Kay–"

"It does," Tyl said. Her chest was tight. She wouldn't stop him. Despite their budding friendship, the way he looked at Pan, and the fierceness in him that she admired. She wouldn't stop him if it meant keeping Pan alive.

"Kay..." Pan's eyelids fluttered closed. His shallow breaths slowed.

Kaylen lifted his hands. "Blood for blood." He stared at her. "Do you accept the deal?"

"Blood for blood," she repeated. Her voice shook. "I accept."

Luke lunged forward as Kaylen brought the blade to his throat. Mira cried out. El cursed.

Memory surged through Tyl's mind. She threw up her hands, fingers trembling as she shouted, "*Wait.*"

CHAPTER TWENTY-NINE

A Bargain

"I can't wait," he snapped, the edge of the dagger pressed to his throat. "He's dying, Tyl."

Before him, the fairy-turned-witch exhaled a breath through clenched jaws. She looked as tired as he felt. Drained. Emptied of the magic that might have saved Pan. But this... this could keep him in a world that would be far worse without his eyes, his laugh, his kindness.

Luke stood a foot away from them, having frozen at Tyl's shout. He glared at Kay with betrayal marring his furrowed brow.

"He's not dead yet," Tyl snapped back. She reached out. "Hand me the dagger. Now."

He hesitated. Pan was still breathing, it was true. He felt each rise and fall against his legs. But the breath slowed. As Tyl delayed what must be done, Pan was fading.

"I won't let him die," she said, her voice gentler this time. "You cannot be the one to collect the ingredients."

Kay inhaled a shuddering breath. That was right. The mermaid had been the one to cut Tyl's wings from her body.

Tyl needed to be the one to take his life in exchange for Pan's.

He flipped the dagger, holding the blade as he handed her the pommel.

"You can't do this." Luke limped forward, his voice breaking. "Captain, please."

"It'll be all right, Luke." Tyl glanced at the man before looking back at Kaylen. "Blood for blood."

Kaylen nodded.

Tyl held the dagger in both hands, rising to her knees with a dark, determined glint in her eye.

"But he's not dead yet." And she swung.

The dagger came down faster than Kaylen could have anticipated from such a drained and wounded person, witch or fairy or human. Steel flashed, pain erupted, someone screamed.

Kaylen's hand. His left hand. It thudded to the floor, causing a sickening splash in Pan's blood.

A surge of light burst from the stump where Kaylen's hand and wrist had been. It shone bright enough to blind. He threw his right hand up to block his eyes.

Around him, the crew cried out. Tyl let out a gleeful cackle. And the body on his lap shifted.

Kaylen gave a rueful grin as he shook his head. "You could have said, you know."

Tyl stuck out her tongue. She was in the process of wrapping his left arm. The bandages needed frequent changing, though the healing would speed up once Tyl's regular magic came back.

That would be a good long while from now, and once they were safely far away from Never Land.

"That wouldn't have been nearly as good a trick," she said with a smirk.

She patted his stump, and he let out a yelp and wince.

"Wouldn't have taken so many years off my life, though," Luke growled from where he and the other crew members were loading the rowboats.

Tyl's grin widened. The magic from their bargain, hastily struck and barely balanced, had given her enough to save Pan. But the marks of how much the magic had cost were evident.

For Kaylen, the missing left hand.

For Tyl, more spider-web thin lines of black had appeared, now at her hairline. As though the magic was slowly breaking her apart.

"I hope you won't hate me for thinking it was worth it." Pan's weak voice caused both of them to turn.

He ambled toward them, one hand pressed to his sternum where a gnarled ruddy scab was hidden by his moss green shirt—the only evidence of his deadly wound. The other hand carried a small sack. Standing on his shoulder, Mira held his ear to keep steady.

"No, I won't," Luke replied gruffly.

Kaylen strode to Pan's side. "Let me," he murmured, reaching for the bag.

Pan laughed, winced, and smiled. "I've got it, Kaylen."

"Oh, let him carry it for you," Tyl said with a smirk. "He's got to get used to doing things one-handed. Might as well start with doting on you."

Kaylen flushed. Pan, looking up at him with the fairy still on his shoulder, did the same.

"I don't..." Kaylen swallowed. Why was fighting pirates easier than talking to Pan all of a sudden? "I don't have to carry it if you..."

"No, it's..." Pan grimaced. "I don't mind you..."

Kaylen's stomach twisted into knots. He tried not to notice the way Mira kept looking from him to Pan expectantly.

"Oh for the love of all growing things," Tyl said from behind him, her voice filled with exasperation. "You both tried to sacrifice your lives for each other. Kiss already."

Pan gave a slow blink, his gaze flicking to his life-long companion before returning to Kaylen. He parted his mouth, licking his dry lips.

And in that moment, with those hazel eyes so unsure yet hopeful, realization clicked within Kaylen.

A smile grew across his face. He reached, right hand sinking into Pan's curls as Pan stepped forward, closing the distance between them.

Pan's hands encircled Kaylen's waist, pulling him close. Their lips met, and every ounce of pain from the battle disappeared in a haze of content. Of belonging. Of joy.

Whoops and cheers went up from the crew behind Kaylen. But he barely heard it. Barely heard or noticed Mira's polite request to be moved, and Tyl's laughter as she hurried up and scooped the little fairy off of Pan's shoulder.

His attention was fixed. Locked on the warm honeyed sweetness of Pan's lips. The easy way the two of them fit together. The happiness filling both of them in that moment.

When they broke apart, Pan's smile rivaled the shine of sunlight on the sea.

Chapter Thirty

A New Adventure

"We need to write down these one-handed jokes," Tyl said, leaning on the rail as she watched Luke steer the ship. "I can't remember all of them."

Luke laughed, the sound clear and free as it had been since their friends had kissed on the shore of Never Land.

"Aye. There are a few of us who remember hook jokes, but I don't know if Kay will appreciate those." Luke pursed his lips, a thoughtful furrow in his brow.

Tyl shook her head. "Let's aim away from those, at least for now." She reached up, adjusting the scarf holding her curls in place. It occurred to her that a different style might be necessary for a life at sea.

"We could start on ones about that blasted red coat." El cackled as she dropped from a rope to the deck behind them.

Tyl laughed.

Luke glanced at the slender pixie-blooded lookout. "All clear ahead, El?"

"Aye." She skipped up to his other side. "Clear skies, open seas, and the next port only a few days from us. Should be a good harbor for offloading the Lost Ones."

"You mean finding them homes," Luke said dryly.

El waved away his words. "Point is, there'll be room in the hold for cargo. Treasure-like cargo."

Tyl's thoughts drifted as the other two discussed their route and plans for what might come after the next stop.

Never Land was long behind them now. The fae who lived there would be finding their own way. Without a queen.

Tyl's heart had broken a little when Mira had decided to stay behind. She'd taken on the task of explaining what they'd discovered from the mermaids. That the queen had been stealing magic not only from the fae, but from the island itself.

The little pink fairy had long wanted to see changes brought to the fairy court. Now she had the chance to enact them.

And she'd promised to watch over Tyl's spellwork. Queen Titania's statue would be carefully guarded for as long as the fairies were able.

How long that would be, Tyl didn't know. But the queen would sleep in stone for a long while. Long past the lives of Kaylen and Pan and the rest of the crew.

Tyl stared absently down at the two men standing at the prow. Kaylen's stump didn't have a hook yet, but there were plans to find a smithy who might create something unique.

Pan was happier than she'd seen him in a long while. It was evident in the lightness of his feet, the way he lit up each time he and Kaylen were together.

A pang went through her heart. A thousand questions clattered around in her head. Ones she wouldn't have answers to for a long time.

Pan could still fly. But he'd died. A fact she kept to herself for the time being. In those final seconds the dagger had cut through Kaylen's arm… It had taken more than the bargain to bring him back.

She felt it in herself. In the way her hands trembled and her head ached. Recovery would take more than a few days or weeks. It would take bargains. Deals to build the magic within her. A magic she didn't know nearly enough about.

And she'd felt it in Pan. When her hand had gone to his chest, her roaring laugh of relief echoing through the Hollow, as she'd slammed life back into him. She'd known that life would not be the same.

But would she?

The terror of losing Pan had always been because if he was gone she'd be alone. A lost fairy on an island of fae who didn't understand her and didn't want to.

Pan caught sight of her staring and stuck his tongue out. She did the same back, and he turned to Kaylen with a laugh.

She wasn't a fairy any longer. She wasn't a human. She wasn't even quite a witch, at least not based on what Kaylen knew about them. Witches worked solely on deals. But Tyl had magic beyond that, too.

Perhaps they'd find answers when they found Kaylen a hook.

She shook her head, pulling her gaze from the love birds and staring out at the sea instead.

There was time. A smile pulled at the corners of her mouth. She let it.

The questions would be answered eventually. Until then, she was on a ship with her best friend, surrounded by pirates, off on another new adventure.

For now, that would be enough.

Thank You

Thank you for reading The Old Tales!
You can find C.H. Lyn's complete works at chlyn.com.

www.ingramcontent.com/pod-product-compliance
Lightning Source LLC
Chambersburg PA
CBHW030920060726
47591CB00005B/1619